Every Inch a Cowboy

*Also by Madeline Baker
in Large Print:*

Lakota Love Song
Reckless Embrace
Warrior's Lady
West Texas Bride
Wolf Shadow

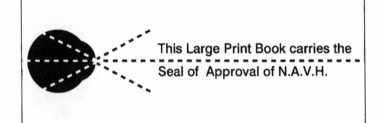

This Large Print Book carries the
Seal of Approval of N.A.V.H.

Every Inch a Cowboy

Madeline Baker

Thorndike Press • Waterville, Maine

Published in 2005 by arrangement with Harlequin Books S.A.

Thorndike Press® Large Print Famous Authors.

The tree indicium is a trademark of Thorndike Press.

The text of this Large Print edition is unabridged.
Other aspects of the book may vary from the original edition.

Set in 16 pt. Plantin by Liana M. Walker.

Printed in the United States on permanent paper.

Library of Congress Cataloging-in-Publication Data

Baker, Madeline.
    Every inch a cowboy / by Madeline Baker.
       p. cm. — (Thorndike Press large print famous authors)
    ISBN 0-7862-7817-X (lg. print : hc : alk. paper)
    1. Large type books. I. Title. II. Thorndike Press
large print famous authors series.
PS3552.A4318E94 2005
813'.54—dc22   2005010523

To the Real
Ashley and Brandon
With hope and love

As the Founder/CEO of NAVH, the only national health agency solely devoted to those who, although not totally blind, have an eye disease which could lead to serious visual impairment, I am pleased to recognize Thorndike Press* as one of the leading publishers in the large print field.

Founded in 1954 in San Francisco to prepare large print textbooks for partially seeing children, NAVH became the pioneer and standard setting agency in the preparation of large type.

Today, those publishers who meet our standards carry the prestigious "Seal of Approval" indicating high quality large print. We are delighted that Thorndike Press is one of the publishers whose titles meet these standards. We are also pleased to recognize the significant contribution Thorndike Press is making in this important and growing field.

Lorraine H. Marchi, L.H.D.
Founder/CEO
NAVH

* Thorndike Press encompasses the following imprints: Thorndike, Wheeler, Walker and Large Print Press.

Chapter One

Dana woke with a groan after a long and restless night. Rising, she took a quick shower, then pulled on a bright yellow flowered sundress, hoping the cheerful color would brighten her mood. It didn't.

Feeling sleep deprived and listless, she fixed breakfast out of habit, though she had no appetite for anything but a glass of orange juice and a piece of buttered toast.

Sitting there, she knew she couldn't go to work. She couldn't face her boss and her co-workers, all of whom had been invited to the wedding. Many of her clients were people she knew, people she saw on a regular basis. By now, she was certain they had all heard that her fiancé, Rick, who was vice president of one of her company's best accounts, had run off to Las Vegas with his secretary.

Her mind in turmoil, she drank the last of the orange juice, took a bite of toast and threw the rest in the garbage. It had been a year since she'd had any time off. Her vacation was overdue and now seemed like the perfect opportunity to take some time off from work. She knew her father would call it cowardly of her to run away at a time like this. He would tell her to stay and face the music, chin up and all that, but she couldn't do it. She just couldn't, at least not now. She needed some time alone, time to sort out her thoughts. Time to come to grips with the fact that she was never going to trust another man and that she was probably never going to get married, never be swept off her feet by a handsome knight on a white horse. Because you couldn't trust knights, either. Even Lancelot had been a tarnished cavalier.

Certain that she was doing the right thing, she called work and told Mr. Goodman that an emergency had come up and that she needed to take two weeks off before the wedding in addition to the week she was already taking for her honeymoon. Since she was a valued employee and she hadn't had a vacation in over a year, her boss reluctantly agreed. Next, she called her mother and told her what had happened. Hearing the sympathy and understanding in her mother's voice brought quick tears to Dana's eyes.

"I'll take care of everything," Marge Westlake said. "Where are you going?"

"I thought I'd go up to the mountains." Dana had a small house in the foothills that her grandmother had left her. Though the house was only a few hours away, it had been years since Dana had gone there. Now it beckoned like a haven of safety, a place where she could hide and lick her wounds.

"That's a wonderful idea, dear," her mother said. "You just go and relax and don't worry about a thing."

"Thanks, Mom. I love you."

"I love you, too."

"Tell Dad I'm sorry . . ."

"Pish posh," her mother said airily. "Don't give it another thought. Call me when you get there."

"All right, Mom. Thanks again."

After hanging up, Dana packed her bags, dumped them in the back seat of her Toyota and left town. It was a beautiful day for a long drive. The sky was blue, the air warm but not hot. Rolling down the window, she turned on the radio, then settled back in her seat and focused all her attention on the road, determined not to think of the reason why she was going up to the Hollow. . . .

Gradually, the city fell behind. Neat houses and strip malls gave way to scattered ranches and stands of timber. Tall pines lined both sides of the road.

Some time later, she turned off the freeway and onto the winding road that led to Wardman's Hollow, Montana. As she drove down the main street, she was glad to see that the old part of town hadn't changed much since she had been there three and a half years ago. Old Town looked just as she remembered it. Long low buildings built of wood and native stone lined both sides of the street. Hitching posts still stood in front of some of the older buildings, like the Shotgun Saloon and Maud's General Store, both of which dated back more than a hundred years. The newer part of town was as modern as any city in the country, with a Wal-Mart and a Target, and the ubiquitous McDonald's, of course. There were a number of gift shops and restaurants, some dress shops and a movie theater. Wright's Ranch Market marked the end of the older section of town and the beginning of the new. The market had been handed down from one Wright to another for generations.

She passed the Bar W cattle ranch. Like Wright's Market, the Bar W dated back several generations. Cattle marked with the Bar W brand grazed on both sides of the road. A few of the cows looked up as she drove past. The town had been named for Cleve Wardman, who had first settled the place in the late 1800s. The southern edge of the Wardman property bordered a section of Dana's land.

She felt a sense of freedom when she pulled into the front yard. The house looked just as she remembered it. A weathered single-story dwelling with a redbrick fireplace and forest-green shutters, it sat in a small clearing surrounded by towering pines, wildflowers and blackberry bushes gone wild. A covered wooden porch spanned the front of the house. Her grandmother's rocker still sat in one corner.

Switching off the engine, Dana grabbed her handbag and suitcase and hurried up the three steps to the front door. Slipping the key into the lock, she gave the door a shove, then stepped inside.

A fine layer of dust covered everything. Lacy gray cobwebs hung from the corners of the ceiling. She knew the place would have been in much worse condition except that her parents had spent a week here last winter and two weeks the summer before that.

Still, she was glad there was work to do. It gave her a sense of purpose. Then, too, staying busy would keep her mind off her reason for being here in the first place.

It wasn't a large house, but it was solid. Her grandfather had built it for her grandmother when they were first married. The interior was rustic. The living room was painted off-white. Colorful rugs covered the hardwood floors. The windows on either side of the front door faced the east. A rack of antlers hung above the brick fireplace. A bear rug took up most of the floor space in front of the hearth. As a little girl, Dana had listened countless times to the story of how her grandfather had killed that bear.

The kitchen was painted a cheery shade of yellow. White lace curtains hung from the big double window that offered a view of the garage, the backyard and the winding stream where Dana had learned to fish when she was a little girl. Four scarred chairs surrounded an equally scarred round oak table that held many memories for Dana. She had drawn pictures on that table and written letters to her mom and dad when she got older. It was at that table that her grandmother had taught her how to make apple pies and sugar cookies and gingerbread men. There was a laundry room off the kitchen. The appliances in both the kitchen and the laundry room had all been upgraded through the years, though the house still lacked air-conditioning. Two bedrooms, one painted a robin's-egg blue, the other a pale green, took up the back part of the house. A large bathroom with a tub and a shower was located between the bedrooms.

Dana dropped her suitcase and handbag on the floor inside the door, then spent the next two hours cleaning the house. She swept the floors and dusted the furniture. She uncovered the dark brown leather sofa and the matching easy chair. She wiped the dust from the kitchen sink and the counter, polished the stove, plugged in the ancient refrigerator, glad that she had thought to call ahead and ask the utility companies to turn on the gas and electricity before she arrived.

She put clean sheets on the big old four-poster bed, pulled some clean towels out of the linen closet and hung them from the rack in the bathroom. She let the water run in the sink for several minutes. When the rusty water turned clear, she washed the sink, then scrubbed the small, claw-footed bathtub.

When she finished up in the bathroom, she grabbed her suitcase and went into the bigger of the two bedrooms and put her clothes away.

That done, she took a long hot bubble bath, then donned a pair of comfortable old sweats and a pair of Reeboks that had seen better days. She brushed her hair until it snapped and crackled, then tied it back in a ponytail.

Returning to the kitchen, she pulled a pad of paper and a stubby pencil out of one of the drawers, and then sat down at the round oak table that had been made by her grandfather. Blowing a lock of hair from her forehead, she began writing out a grocery list.

She felt almost cheerful as she drove to the store. For the next three weeks, she would hide out in her house in the woods and lick her wounds. She wouldn't think about work, she wouldn't think about her poor mother returning all those wedding gifts, she wouldn't think about Rick and his new love. She would simply relax and enjoy the beauty of the mountains. She didn't need a man in her life. Lots of single women lived perfectly happy, productive lives. If they could do it, so could she. She just hoped she didn't end up a bitter old lady with a house full of cats.

Chayton Lone Elk rested one shoulder against the side of the barbershop, a cigarette dangling from the corner of his mouth as he waited for Ashley and her friends to come out of the Sunset Boutique across the street.

Shifting from one foot to the other, he glanced at his watch, wondering what the devil they could be doing in there that was taking so long. Ashley was the boss's daughter and if she wanted to spend all day in town, there wasn't a thing Chay could do about it. Lord save him from giggly teenage girls, he thought sourly. To Chay's dismay, Big John had decided Chay should act as chaperon for as long as Ashley's friends decided to stay. As near as Chay could tell, they didn't plan to leave any time soon. They had already been at the ranch for three weeks and it had been the longest three weeks of Chay's life. Sometimes he thought if he had to endure what they called music for one more day or listen to one more minute of their silly chatter, he would go stark raving mad. Boys and clothes, clothes and boys, it was

15

all they talked about. The only thing keeping him sane was the fact that school started in another couple of weeks.

Chay shook his head as he glanced at his watch again. He figured it was a safe bet that his charges would be in the boutique at least another twenty or thirty minutes, plenty of time for him to run over to Wright's and pick up a carton of cigarettes and then go grab a beer at the Shotgun Saloon.

Tossing his cigarette away, he crossed the street and went into the market.

Betty Wright smiled at him as she rang him up. She was a pretty woman in her mid-thirties with short, curly auburn hair, twinkling brown eyes and a pixie grin.

She shook her head as she bagged the carton. "Chay, don't you know these things will kill you?"

"We all gotta die sometime."

"You really should quit smoking."

"I know. And I will, too, just not this week."

Betty looked at him and laughed. It was the same conversation they had every time he came in to buy a box of Marlboros.

Chay was coming out of Wright's a few minutes later when he heard a muffled crash followed by a soft oath. Glancing over his shoulder, he saw a pretty, young woman in the parking lot. The handle on one of her plastic grocery bags had broken and a dozen or so boxes and cans were rolling around at her feet.

"Here," Chay said, hurrying toward her. "Let me give you a hand."

"I can manage." Stooping, she picked up three of the cans and tossed them in the trunk.

"I'm sure you can," Chay remarked. Reaching under her car, he scooped up five cans of assorted vegetables and deposited them in the trunk with the others.

Dana studied the stranger out of the corner of her eye as he picked up the last couple of cans. He was tall, well over six feet. He had broad shoulders beneath his dark blue shirt, the sleeves of which had been cut off, exposing muscular arms browned by the sun. Fine lines fanned out from the corners of his eyes. A pair of faded blue jeans hugged unbelievably long muscular legs. His thick black hair fell past the collar of his denim shirt. He was, without doubt, the most blatantly handsome man she had ever seen. Next to him, Rick Matheson looked like a washed-out, ninety-eight-pound weakling.

"Thank you, Mr. . . ." She couldn't stop

17

staring at him. Lean and rugged, he looked every inch a cowboy, from the crown of his black Stetson to the soles of his scuffed leather boots. But it didn't matter if he was Mr. America and Brad Pitt all rolled into one. She had sworn off men forever.

"Chay. Chayton Lone Elk."

"Thank you for your help, Mr. Elk," she said stiffly.

Chay watched as she slid behind the wheel and drove out of the parking lot. Who was she? he wondered. He had never seen her before, he would bet his best horse on that. Of course, she might just be passing through, but if that was the case, why was she stocking up on groceries? More likely she was new in town. Maybe she was the new owner of the old Longworth place over off Three Mile Road.

With a shrug, he walked back to the bar-bershop, the beer he had intended to have forgotten. There were too many pretty girls in the world to worry about one little golden-haired female he didn't even know and would likely never see again.

Taking up his place outside the barbershop, he pulled a pack of cigarettes from the carton and lit up.

She'd had the prettiest blue eyes he had

ever seen. The prettiest, and the saddest.

He tried to put her out of his mind, but he was still thinking about her when he drove Ashley and her friends back to the ranch later that afternoon.

Dana stared out the front window as lightning zigzagged across the skies, followed by a long rolling boom of thunder that sounded as if it was going to come right down through the roof. Rain fell in icy sheets. A fierce wind rattled the windows and flattened the grass. The trees bowed before its power.

Turning away from the window, she added more wood to the fire crackling in the hearth. The electricity was out and the only light in the house came from the fireplace and a few candles.

She was glad the stove was gas and not electric as she filled a saucepan with milk and put it on the stove to heat.

Going to the kitchen window, she pulled the curtains aside, though there was little to see but darkness. She had always been afraid of storms, yet she was drawn to them just the same, fascinated by the power of the wind and the rain. She loved the thunder, but she had been afraid of the lightning that scorched the heavens for as long as she could remember.

She gasped as a jagged bolt rent the skies. In the distance, a tree went up in flames. She leaned forward. Was she imagining things, or had she seen a man out there in the rain? With a shake of her head, she drew back and let the curtain fall into place. She had to be seeing things. People didn't go horseback riding in the middle of a storm.

Frowning, she stirred the milk in the pan, then pulled her favorite mug and a box of hot-cocoa mix from the cupboard. She added a couple of teaspoons to the cup and then, as though drawn by an invisible hand, she went to the window, pulled back the curtains and peered outside again.

Another bolt of lightning revealed that there was indeed a man outside. He was slumped over the withers of his horse. Good Lord, what man in his right mind would be out on a horrible night like this? And what was he doing in the middle of her backyard?

Closing the curtains, she moved away from the window, one hand at her throat.

What should she do? Suddenly aware that the milk was overheating, she went to the stove and turned off the fire and then, moving cautiously, she looked out the window once again.

She could barely make out the shape of the horse. It was standing in the same place as before, its head down. There was no sign of the man. Where had he gone? Was he trying to get into her house, even now?

What should she do?

There was a gun on the top shelf of the kitchen cupboard. It was a reproduction of a Colt .45 that belonged to her father. Dana's mother hated guns and refused to let her husband keep it at home. She had refused to let Dana's father teach Dana how to handle the weapon. In spite of that, Dana's father had taken her into the woods and taught her how to load and fire the Colt. She was glad now that he had done so. Of course, she had never fired at anything except targets.

Her hand was shaking as she picked up the Colt. After checking to see if the gun was loaded, Dana went to the window again. The horse hadn't moved. It stood with its head down, its back to the wind. And then, in a flash of almost blinding light, she saw the man. He was lying facedown in the mud. Was he hurt? Dead? Drowning in the rain?

21

Dana watched him for several moments, and when he didn't move, she ran out the back door, her slippers squishing in the mud. Slipping the gun into the oversize pocket of her bathrobe, she turned him over.

Another flash of lightning revealed a jagged gash on the right side of his head, just above his ear.

"Mister?" She shook his shoulder. "Mister?"

He groaned softly as his eyes opened.

"Can you hear me?" she asked anxiously.

A soft grunt was her only answer.

"You'll have to stand up," she said. "I can't carry you."

He muttered something she didn't understand.

Assuming he was agreeing with her, she took hold of his arm and pulled. He sat up, then rolled onto his knees. Using her hand for support, he managed to get to his feet.

Wondering if she was doing the right thing, Dana put her arm around his waist and headed for the back door. It was like trying to move a tree. He towered over her. His arm, resting on her shoulder, felt like a lead weight.

Her slippers were ruined, the hem of her robe covered in mud, by the time she got him into the kitchen. She left her slippers outside, kicked the door shut with her heel. One-handed, she pulled a chair out from the table and he dropped into it.

Now that the rain was no longer washing it away, blood oozed from the cut in his head and dripped down onto the collar of his sheepskin jacket. He was soaked to the skin. Grabbing a dish towel, she pressed it against the wound.

"Can you hold that there for a moment?" she asked.

He nodded, his hand replacing hers on the towel. She frowned, thinking he looked vaguely familiar. She was tempted to ask him who he was and what he was doing riding around on a night like this, but decided her questions could wait. The man was bleeding, after all.

She eased him out of his jacket and hung it on a hook beside the back door, unmindful of the puddle that quickly formed beneath it. She helped him out of his shirt and T-shirt, pulled off his boots and socks, and tossed them aside. Going into living room, she grabbed a blanket from the back of the sofa. Returning to the kitchen, she draped it over his shoulders, then went into the bathroom to see what kind of first-aid supplies she could find.

The medicine cabinet was woefully inadequate. A box of gauze pads, a roll of adhesive tape, a tube of first-aid cream, a bottle of aspirin. She hoped it would be enough.

She stopped in the bedroom long enough to pull on a pair of thick socks and change out of her wet bathrobe and nightgown and into a pair of sweats.

Returning to the kitchen, she dropped the items she had collected on the table, then removed the dish towel from his head. The cut was about three inches long and looked very deep. She was afraid he needed more care than she could give him.

"Just sit tight," she said, replacing the towel. "I'll get my purse and keys and drive you to the hospital. I think you might need some stitches."

"Doesn't matter what I need," he said. "We're not going anywhere. The bridge is out."

"Are you sure? Well, it doesn't matter. There must be another road."

"No."

"Are you saying we're stuck here?"

" 'Fraid so."

She bit down on the inside of her cheek. She was sorely afraid that the first-aid instruction she had received when she was a

Girl Scout wouldn't do her much good now.

He looked up at her, his dark brown eyes dulled with pain. "You got any whiskey?"

She shook her head. "Sorry, I don't drink." Going to the sink, she filled a glass with water, shook three aspirin out of the bottle and handed them to him.

"Whiskey would be better," he muttered wryly.

He swallowed the tablets and drained the glass, then set it on the table. Closing his eyes, he swore softly, and removed the towel from his head. He explored the wound with his fingers, then pressed the towel against his head once more.

"Do you think you can stitch it up?"

Dana stared at him. "Who, me?" She shook her head. "I don't think so."

"You know how to sew, don't you?"

"Yes, but you're not asking me to make you a shirt."

He started to smile, then grimaced. "If you can't do it, I can. Just thread a needle for me."

"You?" she exclaimed, horrified by what he was suggesting. Stitch his own wound? That was the stuff of movies.

"I've done it before."

In the end, she agreed to stitch up the

25

wound rather than have him think she was too chicken, though why she cared what he thought about her was beyond her comprehension. She didn't even know the man. And didn't want to. She'd had enough of men to last a lifetime.

She found a needle and thread and since she didn't have any disinfectant, she turned on one of the burners and passed the needle through the flame, although she wasn't sure what good that would do, since there were probably germs on the thread. She gathered up a dozen candles and placed them around the room for light, setting the biggest one in the middle of the table.

"Sure wish you had some whiskey," he muttered as she sat down beside him.

"Me, too." Even though she didn't drink, she was certain a shot of straight whiskey would help to steady her hand and calm her nerves. "Okay, hold still. I'm sure this is going to hurt you a lot more than it does me."

"I'm sure it will," he muttered, and closed his eyes.

Taking a deep breath, Dana closed her mind to the fact that she was sewing human flesh. She was always reading news stories about people who had done things far beyond what they thought impossible because there was no one else to do it. She was about to find out if she was one of them.

Murmuring a silent prayer for strength and a steady hand, she bent her head to her task.

After what seemed like hours, but was more like twenty minutes, she took one last stitch and tied off the thread. Not too bad, she thought. Still, it was a nasty wound. What if he had a concussion?

She taped a gauze pad over the stitches, then went to the sink and washed her hands. She pulled a clean towel from the drawer, dried her hands, then glanced at her patient to find him watching her.

"You should get out of those wet . . . ah, trousers," she suggested.

He made a soft sound of agreement and rose to his feet.

Her eyes widened when he began to unfasten his jeans.

"Wait! I didn't mean here. You can undress in the spare room. There's a bed in there, too." She studied him a moment, noticing how pale he looked. "Do you think you can make it on your own?"

"Sure." He took a step forward, staggered, and caught hold of the back of a chair.

"Oh, yeah," she said dryly, "you don't need any help at all."

Slipping her arm around his waist, she helped him down the hall to the back bedroom. She was practically carrying him by the time they got there. Sweat dripped from his forehead. His chest was sheened with perspiration. Had she been interested in such things, she would have said that it was a very nice chest.

"Hold still," she said. Then, trying to ignore what she was doing, she unfastened his jeans and dragged the wet denim down over his long, long legs.

She glanced at his briefs. They were wet, too, but if he wanted them off, he was on his own. She helped him into bed and drew the covers over him.

He was asleep as soon as his head touched the pillow.

She stared down at him for several moments, thinking how handsome he was. And then she realized why he looked so familiar. He was the cowboy who had come to her aid in town that afternoon.

Chapter Two

Muttering a mild oath, Chay kept his eyes closed in an effort to ignore the naggingly insistent voice that was demanding he open his eyes.

"Mr. Elk? Mr. Elk! You've got to wake up."

With a low groan, he opened his eyes. Squinting against the flickering light of the candle on the bedside table, he stared at the woman kneeling beside the bed. "Dammit, woman, go away and let me sleep!"

"Do you know who you are?"

"What?" He looked at her as if she was one flake short of a bale. "Is that why you woke me up? To ask me who I am?"

"Yes. What's your name?"

"Go away."

"Do you know where you are?"

He glanced around the room. The walls were sea green; green-and-white flowered curtains hung at the window.

"Your bed?" he asked hopefully.

Her cheeks turned a pretty shade of pink. "In your dreams!"

"A man can hope."

"You're not helping! What's your name?"

"Chay."

"Does your head hurt?"

He snorted softly. "What do you think?"

"Do you feel sick to your stomach?"

"No. Listen, I'm fine. Just a little tired." He stared at her. He recognized her now, the uptight woman from town. Amazing how different she looked with her hair down. It fell over her shoulders in riotous waves of honey-gold silk. Her eyes, those eyes he hadn't been able to forget, were bluer than a robin's egg and still the prettiest eyes he had ever seen, even now, when she was regarding him with what could only be described as resentment. In spite of the fact that she had taken him in and stitched him up, it was obvious she didn't want him there.

"Thank you, ma'am, for looking after me," he said, easing into a sitting position. "If you'll bring me my clothes, I'll get the hell out of your way."

"What? You can't go out in this storm."

"I can, and I will."

"But . . ."

Chay swung his legs over the edge of the mattress, grimacing as pain lanced through the side of his head. "I make it a point never to stay where I'm not wanted, ma'am."

"Stop calling me that," she said waspishly.

"I don't know what else to call you."

"My name is Dana Westlake."

"Sorry to be such a bother, Miss Westlake. If you'll just tell me where my clothes are, I'll get out of your hair." He stood up, then made a grab for the bedpost as the room began to sway around him.

Lunging forward, Dana grabbed his arm to steady him. "You're not going anywhere except back to bed."

"Yes, ma'am," he said, and fell back on the mattress. "Sorry," he said with a lopsided grin. "It just slipped out."

Fighting back the urge to smile, Dana pulled the blankets up to his chin. She was turning away from the bed when his hand snaked out and caught hers. His palm was callused, his fingers long and strong. The touch of his hand sizzled through her like a bolt of lightning.

"What do you think you're doing?" she asked sharply.

"Thanking you for stitching me up," he

31

replied, bemused by the electricity that had arced between them the moment his fingers closed around hers.

Dana stared at the hand holding hers lightly but firmly. It was big and brown, the back crisscrossed with tiny white scars. She was startled by the wave of heat that ran from her palm to her heart as his grip tightened. "Let me go."

"Sorry, Miss Westlake, I didn't mean to frighten you."

"You didn't. I . . . I just don't like being touched."

"By me? Or by men in general?"

She glared at him, wondering why she found him so attractive. Hadn't Rick taught her anything? With a sigh of self-disgust, she jerked her hand out of his, then turned on her heel and left the room.

Chay stared after her, wondering what he had done to upset her. Wondering why he cared. Women didn't usually treat him as if he was dirt. Even though he didn't consider himself to be particularly good-looking, he had never had any trouble attracting the opposite sex. Girls and women alike had come on to him since he turned fourteen. And being a man who liked women, he did what he could to make them happy. He'd had his pick of girls, first in school and later on the rodeo circuit, and now in town.

But this woman looked at him as if he were some kind of vermin.

He laughed softly. There was always one stray in the herd. Still, her standoffish attitude brought out the hunter in him. For some reason he didn't understand, he wanted to make pretty Miss Dana Westlake smile, wanted to hear her laugh. He wanted to run his hands through the honey-gold wealth of her hair, feel her body pressed close to his.

He followed that thought to sleep.

Dana sat at the kitchen table, a cup of hot coffee cradled in her hands. A glance at the clock showed it was a few minutes after nine. Her mind felt like mush. Fearing that her patient might have a concussion, she had set her alarm to wake her every hour through the night so she could check on him. It was a toss-up as to which of them had been more irritable the last time. She didn't know the man and didn't want him here, but here he was and, right or wrong, she felt a sense of responsibility for his welfare.

Earlier that morning, she had tossed his clothing and her robe and nightgown into

33

the washing machine. She had returned the Colt to the top shelf of the cupboard.

Drinking the last of her coffee, she carried the cup to the sink and rinsed it. A glance out the window showed the horse was still standing in the yard. Reins dragging, it was nibbling on a patch of grass, apparently oblivious to the wind and rain. Chay's hat made a splash of black in the gooey brown mud. She felt a twinge of guilt for leaving the animal outside the night before and then shook her head. The horse didn't look any the worse for spending the night in the open. His wild cousins had managed to survive in similar weather. Surely one night in the rain wouldn't hurt this one.

Her heart fluttered in her chest when she heard footsteps behind her. It could only be her houseguest. Turning, she saw him standing in the doorway. He had wrapped one of the blankets around his lean waist. Knowing he wore nothing underneath but a pair of briefs made her mouth go dry.

He jerked his chin toward the stove. "Think I could have a cup of that coffee?"

With a nod, she waved a hand toward the table. "Sit down and I'll pour you a cup."

She took a clean mug from the shelf,

filled it and then refilled her own. When she handed him his cup, she was careful to make sure their hands didn't touch.

"Thanks. Is my horse still here?"

"Yes. Outside," she said, and then felt herself blush. Where else would his horse be?

"I need my clothes."

The memory of helping him undress the night before made her cheeks grow hotter. "They're in the dryer. I'll get them."

Hurrying into the laundry room, she pulled his clothing and her gown and robe from the drier. Seeing his jeans tangled up with her robe caused a funny feeling in the pit of her stomach. She shook out his shirt and jeans, folded his socks and T-shirt, her nightgown and robe, and then, taking a deep breath, she returned to the kitchen.

"Here." She handed him his clothing.

"Obliged." Rising, he left the room.

Dana stared after him, bemused by her feelings for a man she didn't even know. And then she shrugged. It was probably just a case of old-fashioned lust combined with her concern for his welfare. After all, she had taken care of him last night, which explained her concern. And even though she had sworn off men forever, that didn't mean she couldn't appreciate a good-looking man when she saw one. And this man was far too good-looking for her peace of mind! She assured herself that any woman looking at him clad in only a blanket would have felt the same rush of feminine appreciation for his wide shoulders and broad chest.

She was still standing there when he returned a few minutes later. Picking up his cup, he finished his coffee, then turned toward the back door.

"Where are you going?"

"To look after my horse."

"It's still raining. I don't think you should go out. I'll take care of it."

He looked skeptical. "What do you know about horses?"

"Not a thing," she said, though that wasn't entirely true. She knew how to ride.

"That's what I thought. I'll take care of her." Moving slowly, he plucked his jacket from the hook. "Thanks again for stitching me up."

"You're welcome."

He studied her a moment before he shrugged into his jacket and went outside.

She stared after him, wondering if he was coming back. With a shrug she opened the refrigerator and pulled out a couple of eggs and a package of sausage, wondering if Chay liked French toast, and then wondering what difference it made. She wasn't cooking for him. She looked at the two eggs in her hand and put them in the sink. After a moment she picked up four more.

She was surprised when, twenty minutes later, the back door opened and he came in.

He took off his jacket and hung it on the hook, along with his hat. They both dripped water onto the floor. To her surprise, she didn't even mind.

Wordlessly she handed him a towel so he could dry off. A corner of his mouth turned up in a half smile as he took it from her hand.

"Looks like it's gonna rain all day." He tossed the towel over the back of a chair, then sniffed the air. "Something sure smells good."

"French toast, scrambled eggs and sausage," she said, uncovering a platter. "Sit down. What do you want to drink? I've got coffee, milk or orange juice."

"Coffee's fine."

She refilled his cup, poured herself a glass of orange juice and sat down at the table across from him. He helped himself to three slices of French toast and six pieces of sausage.

She wondered if she should have made more.

Silence stretched between them, taut as an electric fence, so strong it was almost tangible. She couldn't seem to stop looking at his hands, wondering what they would feel like on her skin. The thought brought a rush of heat to her cheeks.

"So, what brings you to the Hollow?" he asked after a while. "You on vacation?"

"Yes."

"For how long?"

"A few weeks."

"They're having a barn dance in town next week. Would you like to go?"

"No, thank you."

He grunted softly. "Is it just me, or do you dislike everyone?"

"I don't dislike you, Mr. Elk. I came up here to spend some time alone."

"Guess I put a crimp in that, didn't I?"

"It wasn't your fault."

"As soon as I finish up here, I'll be on my way."

"Don't go. It's still raining, and —" she gestured at his head "— you're hurt."

"Don't worry about me — I've had worse. Besides, the home place will be wondering what happened to me."

For the first time, she wondered if he

had a wife, a family, waiting for him. "What were you doing out in the storm last night, anyway?"

"One of the pasture fences was down and a couple of our horses got out. I was trying to find them when the storm broke. This is mighty fine French toast."

"It's the cinnamon. Did you find the horses?"

"No. I'll pick up the search on the way back to the ranch." He took another bite of French toast. "Cinnamon, you say?"

She nodded. "How did you hurt your head?"

"I was on my way back to the Bar W when lightning hit a tree alongside the trail. One of the branches broke and knocked me off my horse. Guess I hit a rock." Swallowing the last bite of French toast, he pushed his plate aside and stood up. "I'm obliged to you for looking after me."

Dana gazed up at him, stunned by an almost overpowering urge to beg him to stay. "Goodbye, Mr. Elk."

He regarded her for several seconds, then he crossed the room and plucked his jacket and hat from the peg. Opening the door, he stepped out into the rain. The closing of the door seemed unusually loud.

She stayed where she was, her hands curled in her lap as she imagined him climbing onto the back of his horse and riding out of the yard, and out of her life.

"Rubbish," she muttered. "You're just feeling maudlin, that's all. You don't even know the man. How can you be missing him already?"

Missing Chay? It was beyond ridiculous!

She shook the thought from her mind. How could she be lonely for a man she had just met? How could she be missing any man after what Rick had done?

Reminding herself that she was through with men forever, even a drop-dead gorgeous one in tight jeans and a cowboy hat, she threw herself into scrubbing the mud from the kitchen floor.

Chapter Three

Chay found himself thinking about Dana Westlake on the long ride home. He wasn't sure why he couldn't shake her image from his mind. Sure, she was pretty, with her honey-colored hair and those big blue eyes, but he had met a lot of pretty women in his time. Some of them came on to him shamelessly because he was an Indian, some liked him because he was a genuine cowboy. But he wasn't looking for a woman, pretty or otherwise, at least not the kind of woman who wanted to settle down and raise a herd of kids. Not just yet anyway.

He found three of the four missing horses grazing along the side of the road about a quarter of a mile from the ranch. After rounding them up, he herded them down the road until he reached a gate in the pasture fence. He opened the gate and the horses trotted on through, as docile as sheep. When he got back to the ranch, he would send one of the men out to look for the fourth horse.

Chay felt the same sense of homecoming and bitterness he felt every time he rode into the yard of the Bar W. Big John Wardman was standing on the front porch, a cigar clenched between his teeth, when Chay rode up. Big John lived up to his name. He stood a good six feet four inches tall and had shoulders as wide as a barn door. He was in his mid-sixties, his thick brown hair just now going gray at the temples. His eyes were as green and sharp as ground glass. As always, tension crackled between Chay and the boss.

"I was just about to send someone out looking for you," Big John said, speaking around the cigar.

"Yeah?"

Big John nodded. Taking the stogie from his mouth, he tossed it into the brass spittoon that had been on the porch for as long as Chay could remember. "I should have known you could take care of yourself."

"That's right," Chay said. "I always have."

Big John's eyes narrowed. He opened his mouth to speak and then, apparently thinking better of it, he turned away and stalked into the house, letting the screen door slam behind him.

Chay stared after him, one hand clenched on the saddle horn. He took several deep breaths, then turned his horse toward the barn.

"Someday, old man," he muttered. "Someday we're gonna have it out."

But not today.

A couple of the cowhands waved to him as he approached the barn and he waved back.

In spite of the trouble between himself and Big John, Chay loved the ranch. It was a part of him, like the color of his skin, deeply ingrained and unchangeable.

Dismounting, Chay tossed the reins over a fence post, and unsaddled the mare. He gave her a good brushing, cleaned her hooves, then led her into the barn. He put the mare in one of the stalls, gave her a bucket of oats and a forkful of hay, made sure she had water, and finally made his way to the bunkhouse.

Some of the cowhands were clustered around the scarred wooden table in the center of the room, playing poker. Chay tossed his hat on one of the hooks beside the door, then nodded to the card players, noting that Vern Kingston was winning, as always.

"You know you're wasting your time working here," Chay told him. "You ought to be in Vegas or Reno raking in the dough."

Kingston laughed. "Yeah, and I'd go in a heartbeat if cowboying wasn't in my blood."

The men at the table laughed at that. Kingston was the laziest cowboy on the place. The only reason he still had a job was because he was a top hand with the wild string.

Miller gestured at the bandage on Chay's head. "What happened to you?"

"I ran into a tree," Chay replied. "Or, more to the point, a tree ran into me during that storm last night. Speaking of which, I found three of those missing broomtails over near Oak Creek." Chay glanced at a lanky cowboy standing on the other side of the table. "Randall, I want you to ride out and see if you can find the other one."

"Sure thing," Randall replied, and headed for the door.

"So," Kingston said, "who bandaged you up?"

"No one you know."

The men at the table exchanged knowing looks.

"You could introduce me," Joe Coffey said, wiggling his eyebrows.

"Not a chance, Coffey Man. She's too good for a brush popper like you."

The men laughed, then turned back to their game.

Chay bummed a cigarette from Kingston, lit up and took a deep drag. He watched the game while he smoked, then tossed the butt in a trash can and headed for his bunk.

Stretching out, he closed his eyes. Dana Westlake was too good for the likes of him, too, he admitted ruefully. She was a classy lady who deserved all the good things in life; he was just a cowhand with little or nothing to offer her. But that didn't stop him from thinking about her.

It didn't take Dana long to realize that once her things were put away, the house aired out, the floors scrubbed, the windows washed, the groceries put away and clean sheets on the bed, there wasn't a lot left to do except take long walks in the woods or sit on the front porch and listen to the radio. She had brought a couple of new paperback books with her, but for the first time in her life, reading held little appeal. Television was out of the question, since no one had ever replaced the one that broke.

She spent Wednesday morning baking chocolate-chip cookies. Later that afternoon she sorted through the drawers and cupboards in the kitchen; Thursday, she rearranged the furniture in the living room.

By Friday she was weary of her own company. Grabbing her purse and keys, she drove into town to buy a small television with a built-in DVD player.

She was standing beside her car while her new television was being loaded into the trunk when she saw Chayton Lone Elk walking down the street in her direction. Her heart did a funny little leap when she saw him and then she noticed the woman walking beside Chay, a pretty, young woman with a little boy in her arms. A little boy with straight black hair and dusky skin.

Chay slowed almost imperceptibly as he approached her. His gaze met hers. He nodded and then he passed by, his attention again focused on the woman at his side.

Dana stared after him for several moments and then, realizing what she was doing, she jerked her gaze away. She thanked the young man who had put the television in her car, closed the trunk and slid behind the wheel.

So, he had a wife and a child. Why was that so surprising? He was as handsome as the devil, with his coppery skin, long black hair and those sexy eyes that were so dark a brown they were almost black. And it didn't matter one bit. She didn't want a man, any man.

She told herself that all the way home.

She was sitting out on the front porch later that night, sipping from a glass of iced tea while she enjoyed the quiet of the night, when she heard hoofbeats approaching. She knew somehow that it was Chay, though she couldn't imagine what he was doing there.

Her first instinct was to run into the house, turn off all the lights and pretend she wasn't home. But that seemed cowardly and besides, her car was parked beside the house, and her living-room lights could probably be seen for a good distance.

Gathering her courage around her, she continued rocking.

He rode up a short time later, giving her a chance to notice how well he sat his

47

horse, the spread of his shoulders, his clean profile beneath the brim of his hat. "Mind if I light a spell?"

She made a vague gesture. "Suit yourself."

He swung out of the saddle. Tossing the reins over the hitch rack, he climbed the stairs. Standing, he towered over her.

"Sit down," she invited, gesturing at the chair beside the rocker.

Chay folded his length into the ladderback chair, his long legs stretched out before him. "Nice night," he remarked. Reaching into his shirt pocket, he pulled out a pack of cigarettes.

"I'd rather you didn't smoke," she said.

With a grunt, Chay tucked the pack back into his pocket. He had a feeling he'd just given up smoking for good.

"How's your head?"

"Healing pretty well, thanks to you."

"Would you care for a glass of iced tea?"

"Sure. Thanks."

Rising, she went into the kitchen and poured him a glass, dismayed to see that her hand was shaking. What was he doing here, anyway? Why wasn't he home with his wife? She added a few ice cubes, then returned to the porch.

She handed him the glass, shivered when

his fingers brushed against hers. "So," she said, resuming her seat, "what brings you out here?"

"I just wanted to thank you again for looking after me."

"That really wasn't necessary. I would have done the same for anyone."

He grunted softly. She was as prickly as a cactus. "Well, you didn't do it for anyone, you did it for me and I'm obliged."

She shrugged, as if it was of no consequence.

"Tomorrow's my day off," he said, wondering why he was pursuing her so hard when she was only going to be here for a few weeks. "How'd you like to go riding with me in the morning? Maybe have a picnic in the afternoon, do a little swimming at the old water hole?"

"I don't think so."

"I know you came up here to be alone, but I'd really enjoy the company."

"I'm sure your wife would love to ride with you, Mr. Elk."

He stared at her blankly for a moment, and then he grinned. "You mean Kimi? She's not my wife. Just an old friend."

He had known Kimimela since middle school. They had dated some in high school and a few times after that and then she had left town. When she came home a year later, she had a three-month-old baby. Kimi had tried to pass the boy off as Chay's and when that failed, she broke down and cried. She didn't know who the father was, she was all alone and afraid. He had tried to comfort her and one thing had led to another. In the end, Chay had agreed to help support her and her son in exchange for a home-cooked meal and a few hours of companionship on Sunday nights.

It galled Dana that she felt such an overwhelming wave of relief. Married or single, it made no difference. She wasn't looking for any entanglements.

Chay took a long drink and let out an appreciative sigh. "You know, I've been spending a lot of time with a bunch of teenage girls the last few weeks. I sure could use some grown-up company." Seeing the question in Dana's eyes, he added, "The boss has me playing chaperon for his daughter and her friends. He's taking them into the city tomorrow, so I've got the day off."

Dana smiled in spite of herself as she imagined the big cowboy herding a group of giggling teenagers.

"Come on," he said, "have pity on me."

It was tempting. He was tempting. But, remembering Rick, she was about to say no. And then Chay smiled at her and all thought of refusing went right out of her head.

"Pick you up around ten?"

"All right."

"Bring your bathing suit." Rising, he drained the glass. "Unless you want to go skinny-dipping."

He was riding away before she could come up with a suitable reply. Once he was gone, a dozen reasons why she should have refused to go with him popped into her head, but by then it was too late.

She woke early on Saturday morning, filled with a sense of nervous anticipation. She had vowed never to get involved with a man again and now, barely a week later, she had accepted a date with someone she scarcely knew. If she was smart, she would pack up her things and go spend the rest of her vacation with her mom and dad.

But, as she had proved in the recent past, sometimes she wasn't very smart.

She heard hoofbeats outside the door on the stroke of ten. Grabbing the bag that held her swimsuit, towel and a few other

51

necessities, she went out to meet him. Clad in a pair of faded jeans, a dark red shirt, scuffed boots and a black hat, Chayton Lone Elk was a feast for feminine eyes.

Chay smiled as she stepped out onto the porch. "I didn't think to ask yesterday," he said, dismounting. "Do you know how to ride?"

"Yes, though it's been a few years." Shutting the door behind her, she descended the steps.

"I thought you said you didn't know anything about horses?"

She shrugged. "I don't, really."

"Well, once you know how to ride, you never forget. It'll come back to you in no time," he promised. "Just like riding a bike." Taking her bag, he tied it onto the pommel of the second horse, a pretty little chestnut with a white face and one white stocking. "This is Daisy Blue," he said.

"I hope she's gentle."

"As a lamb," Chay assured her. "Come on, I'll give you a leg up."

He adjusted the stirrups, then looked up at her. "You okay?"

"Fine."

A little thrill of awareness rippled through her as their gazes met, only to be magnified when his fingers brushed hers as he handed her the reins.

Chay smiled at her, his expression making it clear that he was aware of what she was feeling.

Dana watched him swing effortlessly onto the back of his own horse. "How far is the water hole?"

"Not far. Maybe forty minutes or so. Why? Are you in a hurry?"

"No, but it's been a long time since I've been riding."

He nodded. "Don't worry, Dana. Is it all right if I call you Dana?"

"Of course."

"Okay, Dana, we'll take it slow and easy."

She felt an unexpected rush of pleasure at hearing her name on his lips. "Why did you ask me to go with you today?"

"I thought I made that clear yesterday. You haven't changed your mind, have you?"

"No."

"Good. Are you ready?"

With a nod, she lifted the reins and the chestnut moved out alongside Chay's horse.

It was a beautiful day for a ride. The sky was a bright bold blue, a cool breeze moved through the pines, keeping the heat at bay. Birds flitted from branch to branch, their songs a cheerful serenade.

Chay had been right. In no time at all, she found the rhythm of her mount, and everything she had ever learned about riding came back to her. She had forgotten how relaxing horseback riding could be. The chestnut had a soft mouth and a smooth easy gait. They had been riding about twenty minutes when they came to a long flat stretch of ground. She nodded when Chay asked if she was ready to let the horses run. Chay urged his horse into a lope and the chestnut lined out behind him.

Dana leaned forward, loving the touch of the wind in her face, the sense of freedom that engulfed her as her horse ran through the tall grass. A deer darted across her path and Dana laughed out loud. Why had she ever given up riding? How could she have forgotten how much fun it was?

Chay let his horse run until it slowed of its own accord. Pulling up, he waited for Dana to catch up with him. Looking at her, it was hard to believe this was the same pinch-faced woman he had met in Wright's parking lot. Her cheeks were flushed, her eyes shining with pleasure.

"This was a wonderful idea," she said as

she drew up alongside him. "How much farther to the water hole?"

"Just around the bend."

It wasn't a water hole at all, but a man-made lake. Set in a verdant meadow, it was surrounded by tall pines and wildflowers. A large wooden raft with an umbrella was anchored in the middle of the water.

Chay dismounted, then turned to help Dana from the back of her horse. She felt a thrill of pleasure as his hands closed around her waist. He lifted her as though she weighed nothing at all. She fought back the urge to run her hands over his biceps.

She looked up at him when he set her on her feet, totally confused by her reaction to him.

Rick had never set her heart to pounding like this, never made her feel warm all over just by looking at her.

"Did you bring a suit?" Chay asked.

She nodded, wishing she dared go skinny-dipping with him.

"Another hope crushed," he said.

"Didn't you? Bring a pair of trunks, I mean."

"Yeah, but I'm willing to swim in the buff if you are."

She wanted to, she really did, but she

just didn't have the nerve. In spite of her attraction to Chay, he was a stranger and she was going home in two weeks.

"Not this time," she said, and wondered if there would be a next time.

"Okay. Men to the left, women to the right."

"Gotcha." Untying her bag from the pommel, she ducked behind a tree to change into her suit, a simple black one-piece. Pulling it on, she wished she had lost that ten pounds she had been meaning to lose, then chided herself for worrying about it. She was what she was and if he didn't like it, what difference did it make? She wasn't interested in winning either his admiration or his affection.

Draping her towel over her shoulder, she took a deep breath and stepped out from behind the tree.

Chay was looking at the water, his back toward her. He wore a pair of navy trunks. Her gaze moved over him in frank feminine appreciation. His skin was a deep copper color all over. His hair fell past his shoulders. He had a tight tush and long, long legs.

He turned as she took another step forward. She felt her cheeks grow warm as his gaze moved over her.

"Nice," he said with a wink.

Her cheeks grew hotter. "Thank you."

He held out his hand. "Ready?"

"Is it very cold?"

"No."

Dropping her towel on the grass, she put her hand in his, felt a rush of electricity flow from his hand to hers as they ran toward the lake and plunged in.

In spite of what he had said, she had expected the water to be cold, but it was perfect. He let go of her hand and she struck out for the far bank, her strokes long and strong, thanks to lessons at the Y. He came up behind her, matching her stroke for stroke.

She was a little breathless when she reached the opposite shore. Climbing out, she sat on the grass while he reversed direction and crossed the lake again.

He swam with ease, drops of water glistening on his broad shoulders, the sunlight casting gilt highlights in his long black hair. She wondered if he did everything as well.

He reached the opposite shore, turned, and swam toward her. She looked up at him as he climbed out of the lake shaking water from his hair, then dropped down beside her.

"It's lovely here," she remarked.

"Yeah. It's always been one of my favorite places."

"Did you grow up around here?"

"Yes."

"On the ranch?"

"Yeah."

"Oh?" There was a wealth of curiosity in that single word.

"My mother used to work for Big John," Chay explained. "She kept his books, stuff like that. She got married ten years ago and moved to Arizona, just outside of Mesa."

Dana remembered Big John. She had seen him one year when she came to stay with her grandparents. She recalled a big, stern-faced man. He had looked at her and scared her half to death. "Why didn't you go with her?"

"No reason to. She didn't need me looking after her anymore, plus I've got a few acres of my own nearby." He didn't mention that his land adjoined Big John's south pasture.

"How long have you worked for Big John?"

"Seems like my whole life." He smiled at her. "How about you? Do you work?"

"Yes, I work for a company that appraises antiques back in Ashton Falls."

"Antiques, huh? I wouldn't think there'd be much call for that kind of work in Ashton Falls."

"You'd be surprised," Dana said with a grin.

"You're pretty far from home," Chay remarked. "What brought you way up here?"

"My grandmother left me her house when she passed away. Talk about antiques! The house, not my grandmother," she clarified.

Chay laughed, and she laughed with him.

"I haven't been up here for several years," Dana said. Leaning back, she braced herself on her hands. "I forgot how pretty it is, how much I've always loved it. I used to come up for vacations when I was a little girl. My grandfather taught me to ride, and my grandmother taught me how to crochet and bake pies."

"What kind of pies?"

"All kinds. Peach, apple, berry, lemon."

"Maybe you could bake me one sometime."

"Maybe."

Their gazes met and locked. Heat flowed through her, as warm and sweet as sun-kissed honey. She swallowed hard. "So, what's your favorite kind of pie?"

His gaze swept over her mouth. "Apple."

He leaned toward her. Suddenly breathless, she stared at him, afraid he was going to take her in his arms and kiss her, and more afraid that he wouldn't.

"Dana."

"What?"

"Nothing, I just wanted to say your name."

"Oh." The thought pleased her more than it should have.

"It suits you," he murmured. And then he drew her into his arms.

"I really don't think this is a good idea," she said, her voice little more than a whisper.

"You're probably right," he agreed. And then, slowly lowering his head, he kissed her. His kiss was like riding the teacups at Disneyland, watching fireworks on the Fourth of July and sitting in front of a blazing fire on a cold winter night all rolled into one.

Closing her eyes, she kissed him back, her arms sliding up around his neck, her body seeking to be closer to his. His skin was warm and still damp and she pressed herself against him, thinking she had never felt anything as wonderful as being in his arms. Never tasted anything as potent as his kisses. Every cell, every nerve ending, sprang to life as his tongue met hers. She wished she had the audacity to take off her bathing suit, to feel the hard length of his body pressed to hers with nothing between them. No man had ever made her feel like this, not even Rick. . . .

Memories of her former fiancé exploded through her mind — Rick holding her in his arms, telling her that he would love her forever, that he would never look at another woman as long as he lived. Ha! Thinking of him cooled her desire as quickly and effectively as a bucket of cold water poured on a campfire.

Turning her head to the side, she broke the kiss.

"Whoa, girl," Chay muttered.

Heat flooded her cheeks. Muttering, "I'm sorry." She tried to wriggle out of his arms, but he refused to let her go.

"Hey, I wasn't complaining." He brushed a lock of wet hair from her cheek.

She looked away, embarrassed by the way she had responded to his kisses. What must he think of her? Another minute and she would have gone up in flames.

Cupping her chin in his palm, he forced her to look at him. "There's nothing to be embarrassed about," he said. "I felt it, too."

"It shouldn't have happened. I'm not looking for . . . for anything."

"Neither am I." He smiled at her as he released her. "Lighten up, Dana. It was just a kiss."

Just a kiss? Was that all it had been to him? She should have felt relieved. Why didn't she?

"Are you ready to swim back?" he asked. "I had Anna Mae, our cook, pack us a lunch."

With a nod, she got to her feet and plunged into the lake. The water felt cool against her heated flesh.

She had regained her composure by the time they reached the other side. Chay found a shady place to spread the blanket. Reaching into the basket, he pulled out roast-beef sandwiches, potato salad, barbecued beans and a thermos of lemonade.

Dana ate self-consciously, unable to forget the way Chay's kisses had affected her.

"So have you ever been married, Dana?"

"No," she said, startled by the question. "Have you?"

He shook his head. "I came close once."

"Were you in love with her?"

"I thought so at the time. Of course, I was mighty young back then, too young to know the difference between love and lust." He looked at her speculatively. "I'm surprised you aren't married. Pretty girl like you, I'd have thought someone would have snapped you up a long time ago."

She thought of Rick. "Just lucky, I guess." At least he had cheated on her *before* they were married. Her friend, Josey, hadn't been so lucky. Well, *lucky* probably wasn't the right word. Ted had cheated on Josey while she was in the hospital having his baby. Men! You couldn't trust any of them.

Chay regarded her thoughtfully for a long moment. "Somebody hurt you, didn't they?"

It was a wild guess, a shot in the dark, but as soon as he spoke the words, he knew it was true. She had been hurt, he thought, and not too long ago if he was any judge. Although he hardly knew her, the thought of some dumb jackass causing her pain filled him with regret. He wasn't sure how he felt about her, but he knew one thing — she was hurting deep down inside and he didn't like it one damn bit.

"I'm sure I don't know what you mean."

"I'm sure you do."

"I don't want to talk about it," she said curtly.

"Whatever you say." He hadn't meant to upset her. He looked out over the lake, giving her time to regain her composure. "I'm supposed to bring Ashley and her friends out here tomorrow," he said after a time.

"I'm sure they'll love it."

"Wanna come along and keep me company?"

"I don't think so." The less time she spent with him, the better. She already liked him far too much. She wasn't getting caught up in that trap again, that wonderful glow of infatuation, the excitement and the anticipation, only to have it all come crashing down around her. No, thank you. She had learned her lesson the hard way. She wasn't making the same mistake again, no matter how attractive she found Chay Lone Elk.

"Come on," he coaxed. "You'll have four of the best chaperons in the world."

She shook her head.

"Are you sure I can't change your mind?"

"Quite sure."

They finished the rest of the meal in silence.

Earlier, Chay had loosened the saddle cinches on their horses. Now, while Dana gathered up their used plates and cups and stowed everything back in the basket, he tightened the saddle cinch on her horse and then his own. Taking the basket, he tied it behind his saddle, and then helped her mount. She felt a familiar warmth slide up her arm at the touch of his hand.

It was late afternoon when they reached her place. Dismounting, Chay lifted her from the back of her horse, his hands lingering at her waist.

Butterflies took wing in her stomach as he leaned forward and brushed a quick kiss across her lips. "Thanks for today," he said. "I had a good time."

"Yes," she said, trying to avoid meeting his eyes. "Me, too."

His gaze found hers and held it for a long moment, then he swung into the saddle and rode out of the yard. He didn't look back.

Standing on the porch, Dana watched him until he was out of sight. In spite of everything, she couldn't help feeling sorry that she would never see him again.

Chapter Four

Too restless to sit down and read, refusing to let herself think about Chay Lone Elk and the time they had spent together the day before, Dana went into the kitchen and pulled out the ingredients for making an apple pie. As she rolled out the crust, she told herself she was making apple because she didn't have the fixings for any other kind. She told herself it was stupid to make a pie when she was going to end up eating it all herself, and that if she wanted to lose that ten pounds, she should be snacking on rice cakes and yogurt. Nevertheless, the fragrant aroma of a pie baking in the oven soon filled the house.

Which again left her with nothing to do. She was tired of watching TV. The bed was made, the breakfast dishes washed and put away, the floor swept and mopped to within an inch of its life, the furniture dusted. Earlier, she had watered the lawn, fed the squirrels, filled the old bird feeder in the backyard. She had done all those things and made a pie, and it was barely two o'clock. She knew now why she liked living in the city, and why she worked six days a week. What on earth did people in the country do with themselves?

The two weeks she had left suddenly seemed like two months.

The pie was cooling and she was thinking about driving into town for lunch when she heard the muffled sound of hoofbeats in the yard. Anticipation fluttered in her stomach. Could it be?

A moment later, she heard the sound of girlish voices and giggles, and then Chay's voice.

"Hey, Dana! Get on out here!"

At the sound of his voice, her heart began beating double time. Still, she forced herself to walk slowly to the front door. She paused with her hand on the latch, took a deep calming breath and stepped out onto the front porch.

Chay was leaning forward in the saddle, his arms crossed on the horn. The horse she had ridden yesterday was on a lead line. Four teenagers were strung out behind him.

"Hey, girl," Chay said, "we came by to see if you'd changed your mind."

Dana shook her head. "I don't think so."

"Daisy Blue misses you something awful," he said with a roguish grin.

Dana's lips twitched in a smile as she glanced at the mare. "She does? How can you tell?"

"She told me so this morning. She said you probably missed her, too, and she begged me to bring her along, just in case you changed your mind. You wouldn't want to disappoint Daisy Blue, now, would you? Not after she came all this way."

As if to add credence to Chay's words, Daisy Blue nodded her head up and down, then whinnied softly.

"You see?" Chay smiled up at Dana, his dark eyes glinting with humor.

Dana laughed out loud, charmed by his words and his smile. What could it hurt to spend another day with him? At least it would get her out of the house.

Chay lifted his head and sniffed the air like a wolf on the scent of fresh game. "Is that apple pie I smell?"

She lifted one shoulder and let it fall in a negligent shrug. "Could be."

"Did you bake it for me?"

"Of course not."

He looked crestfallen. "Well, how about bringing it along?"

"I didn't say I was going."

"Sure you are," he said, and smiled at her again.

Ten minutes later the pie was packed in a basket and tied behind Daisy Blue's saddle, along with a blanket and a beach towel. Dana had taken the time to put her bathing suit on under her clothes and she was ready to go.

Chay introduced Dana to Ashley and her friends, Megan, Brittany and LuAnn. The girls all greeted Dana with cheerful waves and hellos and then they were on their way to the lake.

Ashley was a pretty girl with wavy brown hair and mischievous green eyes. In spite of the difference in their coloring, Dana thought Ashley bore a striking resemblance to Chay.

Chay and Dana rode ahead a few paces. Dana couldn't help smiling as she listened to the girls' chatter. They talked about boys, the latest fashions, boys, which movie stars they thought were really tight, boys, which rock star was in and which was out, whether LuAnn should get a nose ring and what her father, a judge, was likely to do if she did, and boys. It was obvious the girls had been close friends for years, that they were all from wealthy families and accustomed to having the best of everything.

Chay looked over at Dana with a pained expression.

"See what I've been putting up with for the last three weeks?" He groaned softly. "Almost four weeks now."

"You poor thing."

He nodded, his expression woebegone. "Four teenage girls! No grown man should have to put up with such torture."

"Yes, I can see how you're suffering. How much longer are they going to be here?"

He let out a long aggrieved sigh. "Until the end of summer vacation." He shook his head. "I'm never going to get any work done on my own place at this rate."

"What kind of work are you doing?"

"I'm building a house in my spare time." He grunted. "What little I have."

"You're building it? Yourself? Or having it built?"

"I'm doing it — most of it, anyway."

"Wow, I'm impressed."

"Good. Maybe you'd like to see it sometime?"

"Yes, I would. Are you building it for yourself, or for someone else?"

"It's for me. Of course, at the rate I'm going, I'll be an old man by the time it's finished."

"Well, at least you'll have a nice place to live," she said with a grin. "What kind of work do you do for Big John?"

"Cowboy stuff," Chay replied, grinning. "You know, ropin', ridin', brandin', that kind of thing."

"Just like Roy Rogers?"

He snorted softly. "Hardly. Rogers never got his hands dirty. Or his clothes, either."

Dana laughed. "He sure dressed pretty, though — all those fancy clothes. And those boots! I can't imagine any real cowboy wearing red-and-white boots. Of course, the Lone Ranger never got dirty, either. His clothes were always clean and neatly pressed, even after he'd been rolling around in the dirt punching out the bad guy. I always wondered about that."

"You a big fan of the Lone Ranger?"

"Well, to tell you the truth, I always liked Tonto the best."

"Is that right?"

"Uh-huh." She looked at Chay a moment. "You're Indian, aren't you?"

"It shows, huh?"

She nodded.

"My mother is Cheyenne. She was born on the rez."

"How did she happen to go to work for Big John?"

"She left the rez and went to college. She met Big John in a bar one night soon after she graduated. As fate would have it, he had just fired his accountant. He happened to mention he was in the market for a new one during the course of the evening and . . ." He shrugged. "One thing led to another, and the next day she had a job."

"That's quite a story. All it needs is a happy-ever-after ending."

A muscle clenched in Chay's jaw. "Yeah."

"Is your father Indian, too?"

"No." The tone of his voice told her it wasn't something he wanted to discuss.

They reached the lake a few minutes later. The girls were off their horses and in the water in nothing flat, leaving Chay to look after their mounts. He unsaddled the horses, hobbled them in the shade, then removed their bridles, leaving them to graze on a patch of grass.

Dana stripped down to her bathing suit, and spread her blanket on the grass next to Chay's. Each of the girls had a picnic basket tied behind her saddle. Dana lined the baskets up along the edge of the blankets, then sat down, thinking how pretty and peaceful it was with the lake and the trees. The air was fragrant with the scent of wildflowers and grass. A squirrel darted up a nearby pine. Birds flitted from branch to branch.

"You look like you're ready for a swim," Chay remarked.

His gaze moved over her, making Dana wish once again that she had lost that extra ten pounds. He looked ready, too, she thought. His black trunks were the perfect foil for his dusky skin and long black hair. He had never looked more Indian than he did now. All he needed was an eagle feather in his hair and a streak of black paint on his cheek.

Dana glanced at the lake. The girls were playing in the water, splashing and dunking each other and generally having a good time. "Maybe later."

Chay nodded. He sat down on the blanket across from her, his long legs stretched out in front of him, a blade of grass tucked into the corner of his lips.

Dana watched the girls. At twenty-three, she was only a few years older than they were, but she felt years older, certainly wiser. If only she could be that young and innocent again, she thought, worried about nothing more earthshaking than going back to school when summer vacation was over.

73

"Hey." Chay took hold of her foot and shook it. "It's too pretty a day to be looking so serious."

"Sorry, I was just envying them."

Chay glanced at the girls. "I can't imagine why."

She shrugged. "They're so young and carefree. Nothing to worry about except clothes and homework. I wish I hadn't been so anxious to grow up, that I'd enjoyed being a teenager more."

"Does anyone enjoy it?" Chay asked with a grin. "Voices changing. Hormones raging. Trying to find the nerve to ask a girl out. Being scared she'll say no and more afraid she'll say yes. Wondering what to do with her once you've got her alone."

Dana laughed. "It wasn't any easier being a girl, you know. Hoping the right guy would ask you to the movies. Wondering if you should let him kiss you goodnight, wondering how you'd feel if he didn't!" She shook her head. "Maybe I don't want to do it all again."

"Yeah, and it's worse for kids today," Chay remarked. "Drugs on every campus. AIDS. Gangs." Chay looked at the girls thoughtfully, his attention settling on Ashley. She seemed like a bright kid. She would be sixteen soon, a dangerous age for teenagers. He didn't know what he'd do if she got into trouble. He knew Big John didn't pay her much attention. Oh, he made sure she had everything she needed, everything except his affection. Ashley wouldn't be the first girl to go looking for the love she wasn't getting at home in the arms of some smooth-talking young stud who would take her innocence and then dump her. He thought about the promise he had made to Big John. With each passing day, it was getting harder and harder to keep.

"Hey." Dana tapped her finger on Chay's big toe. "Who's looking pensive now?"

He smiled at her, and Dana forgot everything else. The man's smile was more tempting than chocolate, warmer than a wool blanket.

"Sorry," he said.

"It's all right. Tell me about your Cheyenne heritage."

He shrugged. "What's there to say?"

"I don't know. You're the first Native American I've ever met." She frowned. "Do you like being called Native American or Indian?"

"Indian works for me. As for never saying anything outright, I've never felt the need. Anybody looking at me knows who and what I am. If they don't like it, that's their problem, not mine. So, what do you want to know?"

"I'm not sure. All I really know about Indians is what I see on TV and in the movies."

"Yeah, well, most of that is wrong. Indian history was recorded by the whites, not the tribes, so anything you see or hear is likely to be totally inaccurate, either portraying Indians as cold-blooded, godless barbarians or highly romanticized as noble savages."

"What's it like on the reservation? I saw a special on TV a while back. Are reservations as bad as they made it sound?"

"Most of them are pretty grim. Lots of unemployment, teenage suicide, alcoholism."

Dana grimaced. It was not a pretty picture. "Do you go there often?"

"I haven't been back for a couple of years. Since my uncle died, I don't have any family left there and —" he shrugged "— I miss it sometimes. I've got some good memories of the place, and some bad ones, too."

"I used to love movies about the Old West. All those handsome cowboys. Of course, it was the Indians I liked best."

"I'm glad to hear that," he said, grinning.

"In the movies it always seemed like such a romantic part of history," Dana mused.

"I'm sure it was a good way to live," Chay said, "until the white eyes showed up and ruined everything." He smiled at her. "Present company excepted, of course."

As hard as it was to believe in this day and age, there was still some animosity between the whites and the Indians. Chay hadn't experienced much prejudice in Wardman's Hollow, but he'd been subjected to some nasty looks and snide remarks in other parts of the country. He'd taken offense when he was younger; these days he mostly let it slide.

"Of course. I read somewhere that the Cheyenne were considered the most handsome people of all the tribes."

Chay grinned broadly. "Is that right?"

She nodded. "I don't know, though . . ." She tilted her head to one side, her eyes narrowing as she studied him from head to foot. "Not bad. Of course, I've never met any other Indians, so I'm really not a good judge."

"Not bad?" he asked in mock indignation. "Not bad! Is that all you've got to say?"

Dana burst out laughing. "All right, all right, whoever said it was right. At least where you're concerned. Feeling better now? Masculinity still intact? Ego stroked enough?"

He laughed with her, then leaned back, his weight braced on his elbows. "Sometimes when I'm riding across the ranch, I wish I'd been born back then, when the land still belonged to the Sioux and the Cheyenne and the Arapaho. A man knew who he was, and what was expected of him."

Dana shuddered at the mere idea. "I'm glad I live now. Life was too unpredictable back then. Too hard, especially for women. I can't imagine how difficult it must have been just to survive. Doing laundry in a washtub or in a river, cooking on a wood-burning stove, making everything from scratch. No hospitals. Giving birth out in the wild." She shook her head. "No, thank you."

"Life might have been harder, but in some ways I think it was more meaningful."

"Maybe, I don't know."

Chay glanced at the girls. "I suppose

78

kids have always gotten into trouble, but it seems to me they had less time for mischief back in the old days. Kids today have too much time on their hands and not enough responsibility."

"Well, you can't go back," Dana said, "so you might as well enjoy it here."

Chay sat up, his gaze moving over her face, then settling on her mouth. "Oh, I like it here just fine," he said with a roguish grin.

"Do you?"

"Uh-huh. You're here."

She felt her cheeks grow warm at his words, felt a flutter of excitement at the look in his eyes, the husky timbre of his voice. Inching forward, he ran a finger along the inside of her calf. His touch sent a shiver of delight racing through her. Heat flared in his eyes.

Dana glanced over at Ashley and her friends, wishing the girls were somewhere else, wishing that she and Chay were alone so that he could take her in his arms and . . . She took a deep breath and quickly changed the subject. "You said something about a swim. . . ."

Chay's expression told her he was well aware of what she was doing. She was about to ask him if he had changed his mind about a swim when one of the girls screamed.

Chay sprang to his feet. His first thought was for Ashley, but she was fine. She was shouting at him, something about Megan. And then he realized he could see only three of the girls. There was no sign of Megan. Ashley and the other two girls were diving underwater and then coming back up.

Damn! Racing toward the lake, Chay plunged in and swam out toward the wooden raft located in the center of the lake.

He didn't waste time asking what happened. Diving down, he searched for the girl.

He saw her near the bottom, her hair waving in the water like strands of black seaweed. Grabbing her under one arm, he jackknifed to the surface.

"Is she all right?" Ashley asked anxiously.

He didn't waste time talking but struck out for the shore.

Dana was waiting for him. "What can I do?"

"Nothing right now." He laid Megan on the blanket and began giving her artificial respiration. By then, Ashley and the other two girls had reached the blanket, their expressions worried as they hovered over Chay. When Megan coughed up some water, the girls all sighed with relief.

Dana wrapped a blanket around Megan to keep her warm while Chay examined the bump on the side of her head. There was little swelling and no blood.

Turning to Ashley, he asked, "What happened?"

"I dunno," she said with a shrug. "We were just foolin' around. Megan fell off the raft. I think she must have hit her head on the edge. Is she gonna be okay?"

"Yeah, I think so." Chay looked at Megan. "You let me know if you feel dizzy or your vision blurs, or you feel sick to your stomach, okay?"

"I feel all right," she said. "Really."

"You girls need to be careful out there."

"We were being careful," Ashley said, somewhat defensively.

"Well," Chay said, sitting back on his heels, "I think Megan better take it easy the rest of the day. No more swimming."

"All right," Ashley said, obviously concerned for her friend. "Come on, LuAnn, Brittany, let's take our towels over there. Megan, I've got yours. Come on."

The girls spread their towels in the sun,

then stretched out on their stomachs, facing each other, their conversation subdued.

"That was a close call," Dana remarked, resuming her seat on the blanket.

"Yeah. Could have been a lot more serious, I guess."

"She doesn't seem any the worse for wear, other than that bump on her head."

Chay sat across from Dana, one leg drawn up, his arm resting on his knee. "I'll be glad when they all go home."

"You'd rather herd cows than kids?"

"You got that right!" He looked at her and grinned.

Dana felt her heart skip a beat as their eyes met. Lordy, but he was a handsome man! His skin was brown all over. Drops of water glistened in his long black hair, dripped down his broad chest. She looked away, sternly reminding herself that Rick had been a good-looking man, too, and that there was more to a man than his appearance. *Handsome is as handsome does,* her mother always said.

Later, after lunch, Megan declared she felt fine and begged to go swimming again.

Chay shook his head. "I don't think so." Ashley looked at Dana. "Can't you make him change his mind?" Dana raised her hands. "Oh, no, you're not getting me involved in this."

"You're a woman," Ashley said. "I thought for sure you'd be on our side."

"Why don't you girls take a walk around the lake instead," Dana suggested.

"We might as well," Ashley said with a decided lack of enthusiasm. "Come on, girls, let's get out of here."

Sullen-faced, Ashley turned away, followed by the others.

"She'll get over it," Chay said, noting Dana's expression.

"I guess. It's just that I was hoping we'd be friends, although I'm not sure why. I won't be here long enough for it to matter one way or the other."

Chay leaned forward, his hand covering hers. "Is there any chance you can stay a little longer than planned?"

"I don't know. Maybe. Why?"

"I'd like to spend more time with you. It'll give us a chance to get to know each other better."

"I don't think so."

"I know you've been hurt," he said quietly, "but . . ."

With a shake of her head, she pulled her hand from his. "Don't."

Chay glanced over at Ashley and her

friends. The girls hadn't gone for a walk. Instead, they were sitting with their heads together, whispering and giggling while they cut the pie Dana had brought. Didn't look as if he was going to get any, Chay thought, though that was the least of his worries.

"Dammit," he muttered, "we can't talk here."

"There's nothing to talk about."

Oh, yes, there is, he thought. But it would have to wait.

Dana stood on the front porch, waving, as Chay and the girls rode away. It was getting to be a habit, she thought, standing there watching Chayton Lone Elk ride out of sight.

The girls had cheered up later, especially when Chay told them Megan could go swimming as long as she stayed close to the shore. Chay and Dana had swum across the lake and back, and then they had packed up and headed for home.

And now it was dusk. When Chay and the girls were out of sight, Dana went inside and got a bowl of grapes, then went back outside and sat down on the rocker, her feet propped up on the porch rail. Two days of horseback riding had left her aching in places she didn't know she had.

But she had to admit, they were the best two days she'd had in a long time, and Chay was the reason. Like it or not, she was drawn to him. And she didn't like it. Even if she wanted to get involved with another man — and she didn't! — it was too soon. The hurt of Rick's betrayal was too fresh in her heart and her mind.

"Does the word *rebound* ring a bell?" she muttered. Maybe that was all it was, just a normal urge to find another man as quickly as possible, someone to stroke her ego and make her feel desirable.

Why did she have to meet Chayton Lone Elk now, when she was lonely and vulnerable and unsure of herself? Why did he have to be so tall and so doggone handsome? Why did he have to have a smile that could melt ice on a winter day, and a voice that made her insides quiver like melted Jell-O? Why did he have to look so darn sexy in a cowboy hat and tight jeans?

She blew out a sigh. Sexy, she thought. Had she ever seen anything sexier than Chay in those black trunks? It just wasn't fair that she had to meet him now, when he seemed so right and the timing was so wrong.

She was about to go back into the house when a movement in the shadows drew her attention. Leaning forward, she saw three does picking their way through the underbrush across from the house.

Reaching into the bowl, she tossed a few grapes toward the deer. They looked at her for a long moment, then, ears twitching nervously back and forth, they emerged from the brush to eat the grapes.

They were so beautiful, with their large delicate ears and big brown eyes. She tossed them more grapes, and still more. Rising, she moved quietly down the stairs. The deer backed away. Dana plucked a handful of grapes from the bowl and held her hand out toward them. They watched her warily for several moments, then the smaller of the three took a step forward.

Dana kept very still as the doe moved toward her, held her breath as the doe gently nibbled the grapes from her hand while the other two looked on.

Reaching into the bowl again, Dana tossed a handful of grapes to the other two deer. The movement spooked all three. With a flick of their tails, they disappeared into the darkness.

Setting the bowl on the porch, Dana took a stroll around the house. The yard needed work. Tomorrow she would have a go at the weeds in the front yard and along the driveway. And then she would take a whack at the dead tree in the back of the house, although she doubted she would be able to cut it down herself.

She paused at the foot of the stairs and gazed up at the sky. At home, she'd rarely taken the time to look at the stars. Now, she noticed the beauty of the Milky Way. She found the North Star and the Big Dipper and the Little Dipper. Dana frowned, trying to remember where the other constellations were located.

She took a deep breath, her nostrils filling with the fresh clean scent of earth and pine. She really did love it here, the trees and the deer and the squirrels. The sky seemed bigger, the stars more plentiful.

Yawning, she went into the house and fixed a light dinner, then, muscles aching, she took a long hot bath. When the water grew cool, she stepped out of the tub, pulled on her nightgown, then grabbed a book and crawled into bed.

She stared at the words on the page, but it was Chayton Lone Elk's face she saw, Chay's image that followed her to sleep.

Chapter Five

"Why the hell weren't you more careful? Dammit, the girl could have drowned."

Chay stood in front of Big John's desk, his hands tightly clenched at his sides as the old man continued the rant that had been going on for the last twenty minutes.

"Well?" Big John spread his hands on his desk and leaned forward. "What do you have to say for yourself?"

"Not a damn thing."

Big John reared back, his eyes narrowing, his face mottled with rage. "Get the hell out of my office."

Turning on his heel, Chay stalked out of the room. He was almost at the front door when Ashley stepped into his path.

"I'm sorry, Chay," she said quietly.

"It's not your fault."

"I know how you hate looking after us. I don't know why Daddy thinks we need a chaperon."

Chay grunted softly. "Today's a perfect example of why you need a keeper," he said, but there was no anger in his voice, only affection.

Ashley threw her arms around him and gave him a bear hug. "I love you."

"I love you, too, kitten."

"I don't know why Daddy's making such a big fuss. Megan's fine."

"We were lucky," Chay said, ruffling her hair. "It could have been a lot worse. Go along now."

"All right." She started down the hallway, then stopped and glanced over her shoulder. "Are you gonna see Dana again?"

"I don't know, why?"

Ashley shrugged. "No reason. She's pretty, isn't she?"

"She is that," Chay agreed.

"Prettier than me?"

"No one's prettier than you."

With a smile, Ashley ran up the stairs.

Needing some fresh air, Chay left the house and headed for the corral. He whistled softly and his horse trotted up, snuffling softly.

"Hey, girl." Propping one foot on the bottom rail, Chay scratched the mare between her ears. "Damn that old man," he muttered. "If I had any sense, I'd pack up and leave this place." But even as he said the words, he knew he wouldn't go. Not only because he didn't want to, but because it would make Big John's life so much easier if he didn't have to see his illegitimate son every day.

Of course, leaving would make Chay's life easier, too. His mother had tried to persuade him to go with her when she married Frank Heston, but Chay had stubbornly refused to go. Big John was his father and Chay intended to stay on at the ranch until the old man acknowledged that fact to the whole damn world. He had spent most of his life trying to make his old man proud of him. He worked harder than any hired hand on the place, and he was damn good at what he did. He could outrope and outride any cowboy within a thousand miles. He understood horses and cattle as well as, if not better than, Big John himself. And then there was Ashley. She was his half sister and she didn't even know it.

Chay gave the mare a final pat. "See ya later, girl."

Turning away from the corral, he headed for the bunkhouse. He waved to the other cowhands, paused a moment to watch a poker game. As usual, Vern Kingston was winning big. Chay knew some of the other men thought Kingston cheated at cards, but Chay had played enough poker with Vern to know better. Kingston wasn't just good, he had the devil's own luck at the game.

Moving on, Chay dropped down on his bunk, one arm thrown across his eyes. He wasn't surprised when Dana's image immediately popped to the forefront of his mind. She tempted him and intrigued him more than any woman he had ever met, and he had met quite a few. But none of them appealed to him the way she did. She brought out his protective instincts, made him want to shield her from life's heartaches, heal the hurt he sometimes saw in her eyes.

"Damn," he muttered irritably, "you've got it bad."

Yet even as he chided himself for being a fool, he was trying to find a plausible reason to go by her place again tomorrow.

Dana sat back on her heels and stretched the kinks out of her back and shoulders. It had been years since she had pulled weeds, especially this many of the sticky little things. She wouldn't have minded so much if scrabbling in the dirt had accomplished its purpose and kept her from thinking of Chay, but it didn't. She was worse than a teenager with her first crush. She thought about Chay and her insides turned to mush. When she was with him, all she wanted to do was touch him, hear his voice, see him smile. When they were apart, she daydreamed about him. She dreamed of him at night, too.

She shook her head. Last night, she had dreamed of Chay. He had ridden up on his horse, swept her off her feet and carried her away to a house located in a green meadow. There had been cattle on the hillsides. He had carried her into the house and shut the door, and shut out the rest of the world. . . .

She pushed the memory aside. It was only a dream, and dreams were for fools. She was a grown woman with a responsible job, not some silly little girl who had just been dumped for the first time.

Only it *was* the first time. And it hurt. And she never wanted to feel this way again.

With a shake of her head, she started tossing the weeds into a plastic bag. As soon as she finished up here, it would be time to fix lunch. She licked her lips, anticipating an ice-cold glass of lemonade.

Half an hour later, the weeds in the front of the house were gone. Rising, one hand pressed against the small of her aching back, she debated going into town and buying some flowers to line the driveway. It seemed like a foolish gesture when she was only going to be there another two weeks. Still, there was something very satisfying about working in the yard and getting her hands dirty. And flowers didn't cost that much.

Another half hour or so, and she would go inside, get cleaned up and drive to the nursery in town.

It had taken some doing, but Chay had finally found an excuse to ride up near Dana's house again. Of course, having the girls with him wouldn't allow for much courting. . . . Good Lord, where had *that* word come from?

Chay frowned as he urged his horse up the slope. Courting! Was that what he was doing? There didn't seem much point in it, since Dana would be going back to Ashton Falls in a couple of weeks, but courting or not, he had to see her again.

He glanced over his shoulder to make sure the girls were all behind him. Megan was fully recovered from her incident of the day before, with nothing to show for her mishap but a small bruise on the side of her head. Chay wished he could say that. He was still seething from the tongue-lashing he had received from Big John.

He waved a hand at Ashley when she looked up. The girls rode two abreast, whispering and giggling. He wondered what teenagers talked about these days when there were no adults to overhear their conversations, and then decided he really didn't want to know.

He felt a quickening inside when they turned up the road to Dana's house. Bemused by his feelings, at first he didn't see her kneeling beside the driveway.

She looked up, apparently as surprised as he was. "What are you doing here?" she asked, waving to the girls.

"They wanted to go berry picking," Chay replied. It was only partly a lie. Berry picking had been his idea, but they had been agreeable.

"Isn't it kind of late in the year for berry picking?"

"This high up there're probably a few left. Why don't you come with us?"

She glanced down. Her jeans were dirty

and so were her hands. And she still had flowers to plant.

"You're fine the way you are," Chay said, reading her thoughts. "Berry picking can be dirty work."

"I don't have a horse."

His gaze met hers, his dark eyes twinkling with mischief. "It's not far. We can ride double."

The look in his eyes, and the thought of riding behind him, her arms wrapped snugly around his waist, sent a thrill of excitement fluttering through her stomach.

"Well, what do you say?" he asked.

The rest of the flowers could wait. "Just let me wash my hands."

At his nod, she hurried into the house, washed her hands, ran a brush through her hair and tied it back in a ponytail. She debated putting on lipstick and decided against it, but then vanity won out. She checked herself in the mirror one last time, then practically ran out the front door.

Chay rode up beside the porch. Offering her his hand, he swung her up behind him.

"Hang on tight," he said. "I don't want to lose you."

His words filled her heart with warmth. Murmuring, "Yes, sir," she slid her arms around his waist, resisting the temptation to rest her cheek against his back.

They rode around the side of the house and up a long narrow trail that opened onto a flat stretch of prairie. Shrubs and tall trees dotted the landscape, as well as a long tangle of wild huckleberry bushes that still held some of the small blue-black fruit. Montana was known for its huckleberry jams and jellies. You could even buy huckleberry-scented candles. Of course, there were some who said that they weren't true huckleberries at all, but blueberries.

Chay pulled his horse to a stop. He offered Dana his hand again and she swung down from the horse's back. Dismounting, Chay gathered the reins of all the horses and tethered them to a couple of trees. The girls each had a straw basket tied behind their saddles. Retrieving them, they moved among the berry bushes, each boasting they would be the first to fill their basket.

"I'll bet they eat more than they collect," Chay remarked, watching them. "Come on, let's go pick a few before they're all gone."

"Sounds good to me."

And they were good. Chay ate a handful but mostly he watched Dana. She looked as young and carefree as one of the teenagers as she laughed with them. His gaze settled on a drop of berry juice caught in the corner of her mouth. What would she do if he pulled her into his arms and licked that tempting drop away? Deciding it was well worth a kiss or a slap, he drew her into his arms and licked the juice from her lips.

Startled, she jerked back, her eyes widening. "Why did you do that?"

"You had juice," he said, touching his finger to her lips, "just there." He smiled at her. "But it's gone now."

"Really?" Lifting her hand to her mouth, she ate another couple of berries. "Do you see any more?"

"Here," he said, kissing the opposite corner of her mouth. "And here." He nibbled on her lower lip. "And here." This was a full-blown kiss that rocked him down to his boot heels.

"Hey, you guys!" Megan called. "We're supposed to be picking berries!"

"Yeah," Ashley agreed. "What kind of example are you setting for us impressionable teenagers anyway?"

With a groan, Chay released Dana and took a step backward. "Maybe this wasn't such a good idea," he muttered.

Dana made a face at him. "Well, gee, thanks a lot."

"No, honey, I didn't mean kissing you. I meant bringing the girls."

"I thought you said this was their idea?"

"Did I say that?"

"Unless you were lying."

"Well, it wasn't a lie, exactly."

"What was it then, exactly?"

"All right, you caught me. It was my idea. I wanted to see you again, and this was the only reason I could think of for coming up this way."

It was hard to be mad at a man who had lied because he wanted to see her again. But it was still a lie. And even though it was just a tiny little white lie, it still bothered her.

Chay lifted one eyebrow. "What?"

"What do you mean?"

"You're upset about something."

"I don't like lies, even little ones."

"Is that what he did?" Chay asked softly. "Lie to you?"

"Among other things," she replied coolly, and turned away from him.

"Hey, hold on a minute." His long fingers curled around her wrist, drawing her toward him again. "Talk to me, Dana."

She glanced pointedly at the girls, all of whom were watching them avidly.

Chay muttered an oath under his breath.

"You're right. This isn't the time or the place." His gaze bored into hers. "But we're gonna talk about this later."

The rest of the afternoon passed pleasantly enough. Dana enjoyed being with the girls, listening while they chatted about which singers they liked best, Ashlee Simpson or Norah Jones, and who had the cutest smile, Orlando Bloom or Johnny Depp. They complained about school and homework and how unreasonable and demanding parents could be.

By four o'clock, the girls were ready to go home. Chay rounded up the horses and gathered up the baskets and in no time at all, they were riding back down the hill.

Dana again rode behind Chay, her senses filling with his nearness. Not only was he the most handsome man she had ever seen, but he was also the tallest and the most rugged. She knew instinctively that no matter what happened, he could protect her. He was also the sexiest man she had ever met, with his dusky skin and long black hair, not to mention his megawatt grin and whiskey-smooth voice.

No doubt about it, she had it bad! And you were through with men, she reminded herself. Ha!

But she couldn't forget he had lied to

her. A silly, harmless lie, to be sure, but then, Rick's lies had seemed harmless at first, too, and look how that had turned out.

When they reached her place, Chay dismounted. Lifting her from the back of the horse, he walked her to her door. "Thanks for coming with us."

"Thanks for asking me."

"I've got to get these girls back. Remember that barn dance I told you about? Well, it's tonight and they want to go." He shook his head ruefully. "Naturally, I've been assigned to be their driver and chaperon." He cocked his head to one side. "You said no the last time I asked you, but how about going with me?"

"I don't know . . ."

He ran his knuckles over her cheek. For a touch that was as light as thistledown, it went through her like heat lightning. "Say you'll go with me."

"I'll go with you."

He gave her a quick kiss on the cheek. "We'll pick you up at seven."

"All right. See you then."

"Good. Hang on a minute."

Descending the stairs, he went to Ashley's horse and removed one of the baskets from the saddle.

"Here," he said, handing the basket to Dana.

"Thanks. I suppose you want another pie, since you didn't get any of the last one?"

"That's the idea," Chay admitted with a grin.

"I thought apple was your favorite."

"I like huckleberry, too. See you at seven."

Chapter Six

Wrapped in a fluffy pink towel, Dana stood in front of the closet trying to decide what to wear. She really hadn't brought anything fancy, but then, she hadn't planned on meeting anyone like Chay or being invited to a dance. In the end, she chose a long navy blue and white flowered skirt that was drawn up on one side, exposing a froth of white lace, and a white blouse. She brushed her hair and twisted it into a knot on top of her head, then shook it down again. She pulled on a pair of high-heeled blue sandals, applied some lipstick, splashed on a little perfume and she was ready to go.

Her heartbeat skyrocketed when she heard his knock. Taking a deep breath, she went to answer the door.

Dana sucked in a deep breath when she saw Chay standing on the porch. He was gorgeous. A pair of new black jeans hugged his long legs. He wore a black leather vest over a white western-style shirt. Both complemented his dusky skin and dark eyes.

He touched a forefinger to the brim of his black hat. "Are you ready to go, ma'am?" he asked in his best cowboy twang.

She batted her eyelashes at him. "Why, yes, I am, kind sir."

He offered her his arm. "Your carriage awaits."

Carriage indeed. Dana's eyes widened when she stepped out onto the front porch and saw a long black limousine waiting for her.

Descending the stairs, Chay opened the passenger door for her.

From the back seat, a chorus of female voices called, "Hi, Dana," as she slid onto the butter-soft leather seat.

Smiling, Dana glanced over her shoulder. "Hi, girls."

Ashley lifted a champagne glass filled with soda. "Isn't this great?"

It was better than great. The windows were tinted, the carpets a plush gray to match the seats. There was a small television in the back, as well as a refrigerator.

"Pretty swanky," Dana said as Chay put the car in gear. "Is it a rental?"

"Of course not. It belongs to Big John,"

Chay said, his reply pitched low for her ears alone. "Like just about everything else in this town."

Dana stared at him, somewhat taken aback by his brusque tone. The bitterness in his voice was unmistakable. "You don't seem to like Big John very much," she remarked. "Why do you work for him?"

"He pays well."

"And that's reason enough to work for someone you don't like?"

He shrugged. "I told you, I've got a few acres here. I run some cattle on it and in another six months or so, the house will be done. It's too much to walk away from."

"You're right, of course. I forgot about the house. I guess it's just hard for me to imagine working for someone I don't like."

"Well, if you've never had to do it, you're lucky."

"Yes," she said wistfully. "Lucky."

Chay pulled up in front of the high school a few minutes later. The girls exploded out of the back of the limo like a covey of quail spooked by a fox.

It was the first time Dana had seen them in anything but jeans. Heads together, they hurried through the door to the gym.

Chay came around to help Dana out of the car. "I hope you like loud music," he said, taking her by the hand.

It had been years since Dana had been to a dance held in a high-school gym. Colorful streamers hung from the ceiling. A long table held bottles of water and cans of Coke. Another table held cakes and pies and cookies. Several adults roamed around the edge of the room, keeping an eye on the kids. Music was provided by a live band. Huge speakers were located at either side of the bandstand. Dana decided loud was an understatement as the singer belted out the latest hit by Alan Jackson.

Chay, Dana and the girls made small talk for a moment, then a tall, good-looking boy sauntered over and asked Ashley to dance.

"That's Brandon DeHaven," Chay said, watching the teenagers melt into the crowd. "His old man owns the spread next to Big John's."

"They look good together," Dana said.

"Yeah. So, how about it?" Chay gestured at the dance floor. "You game?"

"Sure."

The music changed to something sad and slow as he led her out into the middle of the floor and took her in his arms.

"I've never been a country-music fan," Dana said. "Seems like every other song is about broken hearts and starting over."

"Did he break your heart?" Chay asked quietly.

"Are we back to that again?"

"Talk to me, Dana. Tell me what he did to you."

She glanced around. "This isn't the time or the place to discuss it, you know, so why don't you just forget it?"

"I'd like to," he said. "But it's like an itch I can't scratch." Holding her close, he guided her around the floor, his body brushing intimately against her own. "You can trust me, Dana. I won't betray your trust."

"That's what Rick said, in the beginning. He told me that he loved me and he promised that he would never, ever hurt me, or leave me. Only it was all a lie. Everything he ever told me was nothing but a damn lie!"

"I'm sorry, Dana." His voice, soft and low, wrapped around her like a warm cotton quilt. "I'm sorry he hurt you."

"It doesn't matter now. It's over."

"Is it?"

"Yes, and I don't intend to let anyone hurt me again."

"That's no way to live."

"Have you ever been hurt by someone

you loved?" she asked. "Someone you trusted? Did you plan a wedding and buy a dress that cost a month's pay and send out the invitations, only to have the man you loved call you the week before the big day and tell you he was marrying someone else?"

Chay swore. "Is that what happened?"

"Yes." Twisting out of his arms, Dana ducked out the side door and into the darkness beyond before she broke into tears and made a complete fool of herself.

She should have known Chay would follow her.

"Dana, wait!"

She would have kept going, but his hand on her arm stayed her. She blinked back the tears that threatened to fall. "Chay, just let it go."

"I would if I could. I know we just met a few days ago, but you're under my skin."

"Like an itch you can't scratch?" she asked, sniffling.

He laughed softly. "I guess you could say that." He pulled a handkerchief out of his pocket and gently wiped her eyes. "Admit it, there's something between us. At least give us a chance to find out if it's worth pursuing."

"What's the point? I'm only going to be

here another two weeks."

"Then give me those two weeks."

"You're very persistent."

"You ain't seen nothing yet."

She stared up at him. If she was smart, she would pack up and go home tomorrow, before things got any more complicated than they already were. She liked Chay. She was attracted to him, and that fact scared her half to death. She had been attracted to Rick, too, although what she had felt for Rick was like comparing a summer breeze to a hurricane. There was just no comparison. Her attraction to Rick had never been as strong as what she felt for Chay.

His hand slid up her arm to rest on her shoulder. Heat flowed in the wake of his touch. "Come back inside and let's finish our dance, all right?"

With a nod, she let him lead her back into the gym. He took her in his arms again, their bodies moving together as if they had danced this way for years. His nearness did funny things in the pit of her stomach, made her wish that they were alone somewhere. Made her wish for things she had convinced herself she no longer believed in. The touch of his hand at her waist burned through her blouse, spreading heat up and down her spine. She had danced with lots of men, but it had never been like this. Being in Chay's arms was more than mere dancing.

She was sorry when the song ended. Leaving the dance floor, they moved toward the refreshment tables. She chose a slice of cherry pie; he picked apple. Carrying their plates and cups of hot apple cider, they found a vacant table and sat down. While they ate, he entertained her with humorous stories about the local townspeople, all the while keeping a watchful eye on Brandon DeHaven, who seemed glued to Ashley's side.

Dana was struck again by the uncanny resemblance between Ashley and Chay, though she couldn't pinpoint exactly what it was. Their coloring was different, but there was something about their eyes, the shape of their mouths, even the way they carried themselves.

"Hey, girl, where are you?"

"What? Oh, I was just watching Ashley. She's such a pretty girl."

"Yeah, she sure is. She'd most likely be causing her old man a lot of sleepless nights if he gave a damn about her."

"He must care," Dana said. "If he didn't, why would you be chaperoning her everywhere she goes?"

"It's only for the summer. When it's over, she'll go back to school, and I'll go back to being a cowboy."

"So she doesn't live at the ranch all year?"

"No, just summers and during Christmas vacation."

"That's too bad." Dana took a sip of her drink. "Where's Ashley's mother? You've never mentioned her."

"She hightailed it out of here a couple of years ago."

"Why didn't she take Ashley with her?"

"Big John wouldn't let her."

"But if he doesn't really care . . ."

"Big John keeps what he wants to keep, one way or another." Big John had given Chay a thousand acres of prime grassland, figuring that the land and the promise of having his own ranch one day would be the one thing Chay couldn't walk away from. Big John had been wrong about that, he just didn't know it. The one thing Chay didn't understand was why the old man wanted to keep him around. They hadn't exchanged two congenial words in the last fifteen years. It didn't make sense, but then, Big John did a lot of things that didn't make sense. Chay had stopped trying to figure the old man out years ago.

Chay watched Ashley laugh at something Brandon said. Ashley was the only reason he stayed on at the ranch. He could have walked away from the old man. He could have left the thousand acres he owned without a backward glance. But he couldn't walk out on Ashley. She needed somebody on her side, and Chay was all she had. He had loved Ashley from the moment Jillian brought her home from the hospital, had been her slave ever since the day her dimpled fingers first curled around his fourteen years ago. Once she learned to walk, she had followed him around the ranch, wanting to be wherever he was, wanting to do everything he did. He was still living in the main house back then and she was always sneaking into his bed at night. Years later, it had been Chay she had turned to for comfort when her mother packed up and left the ranch, Chay she talked to in the middle of the night whenever something was bothering her. Sometimes he felt more like her father than her half brother.

He glanced at Dana when she tugged at his arm.

"So," she asked, "where were *you?*"

"Just remembering when she used to follow me around like a puppy, copying everything I did. Treating me like I'm her big brother."

"I always wanted an older brother or even a sister, but my mom couldn't have any more kids after I was born. Do you have brothers or sisters?"

Chay hesitated a moment, and then shook his head. As much as he wanted to tell Dana the truth, he couldn't do it. Years ago, Big John had made Chay promise that he would never tell anyone that Ashley was his half sister. Even now, Chay wasn't sure why. He doubted Big John gave a damn what his neighbors or anyone else thought of him. Big John had had a brief affair with Chay's mother. Since then, he had been married four times. None of his wives since Jillian had stayed around more than two or three years. The old man had sworn off marriage after the last one left. The last Chay had heard, Big John was keeping company with Georgia Cookson. Georgia owned a boutique in town. She was a voluptuous blonde, at least fifteen years younger than the old man.

"Sad, to be all alone in the world," Dana murmured.

"Yeah. Looks like the party's breaking up. I'll go round up the girls."

"Okay."

She watched Chay move through the crowd. It was easy to follow his progress across the room; he stood head and shoulders above just about everyone else. Though she couldn't hear what was being said, it was obvious that Ashley and Chay were having an argument. Judging from the sullen expression on Ashley's face as she followed Chay across the floor, Dana guessed Ashley wanted to spend more time with Brandon. Dana couldn't blame her. Brandon was a good-looking, clean-cut kid and seemed very nice.

Once they were all in the limo, Ashley's mood brightened up. The girls laughed and giggled on the drive back to Dana's house, comparing notes on the boys they had danced with, occasionally making catty remarks about some of the other girls.

Chay pulled up in front of Dana's house. Getting out of the car, he walked around the front and opened Dana's door for her.

There were good-natured hoots and catcalls as he walked Dana up the steps to her door.

"Thank you," she said. "I had a nice time."

"Me, too."

"Hurry up and kiss her," Megan hollered.

"Yeah," LuAnn said. "Get it over with so we can go home!"

Chay laughed softly. "What do you say?"

"We shouldn't disappoint them," Dana murmured.

"No," Chay agreed. "We wouldn't want to do that."

Dana looked up at him, her heart beating triple time as he lowered his head. She closed her eyes as his lips claimed hers. Since there were four teenage girls in the car looking on, Dana had expected a quick kiss good-night, but Chay was in no hurry. His lips moved slowly over hers, his tongue lightly stroking her lower lip as his arms drew her body up against his.

Dana leaned into him, grateful for his support as her legs turned to jelly. Her every sense was aware of the man holding her in his arms. She ran her hands up and down his broad back, a shiver skittering down her spine as she felt his arousal. She was grateful she was a woman. She might be every bit as hot and bothered as he was, but at least it didn't show!

She moaned softly, wondering how it was possible for one kiss to affect her so quickly.

She stared up at him, mutinous, when he took his lips from hers.

"I know, sweetheart," he said, his voice low. "We'll continue this some other time when we don't have an audience."

Only then did she remember Ashley and her friends were watching avidly from the windows of the limo.

Chay kissed her again, then, whistling softly, he descended the steps to the car and slid behind the wheel.

Grateful for the shadows that hid her blush, Dana waved at the girls, then stood on the top step, watching the taillights of the limo grow fainter and fainter until they were out of sight.

Chapter Seven

The next morning after breakfast, Dana put on a pair of well-worn jeans, a T-shirt and a pair of boots and headed for the garage. Inside, she found a handsaw and an old pair of work gloves. She glanced around the garage, thinking it could use a good cleaning. There were old tools and boxes piled in one corner along with bits of old tack and coils of rope. But cleaning out the garage was a project for another day.

Pulling on the gloves, she went out to tackle the big old dead tree in the backyard. It was really a foolish endeavor. There was no way she could cut down the trunk or remove the stump unless she called a professional, no way she could cut off the highest limbs, since she didn't have a ladder that was tall enough to reach them. On top of all that, she was only going to be here for less than two weeks, so what did it matter? In spite of all the obstacles, it was something to do.

It took her two hours to saw off four of the lower limbs. She had never been much for hard physical labor, but she found the task oddly satisfying. And since the wood was so dry, it would make great firewood. Of course, she wouldn't have much need for firewood anytime soon, since she would be back home long before winter set in.

Deciding it was time for a break, she removed her gloves and went into the house for an apple and a glass of lemonade.

Sitting at the kitchen table, her thoughts turned to Chay. Nothing unusual about that, she thought dryly, since it seemed that hardly an hour went by when she wasn't thinking of him. Or dreaming of him, like last night. Oh, my, what a dream that had been!

She smiled just thinking about it. They had been at the lake, just the two of them. In her dream, she had found the courage to overcome her self-consciousness and her modesty and go skinny-dipping with Chay. It had been glorious, exhilarating, though she couldn't say why. She was naked when she took a bath, but swimming in the nude was completely different. Maybe it was the feel of the water moving over her nakedness. Maybe it was the touch of Chay's gaze on her bare skin. . . .

She felt herself blush as she recalled how they had made love on a blanket under the bold blue sky. Of course, since she had never gone all the way, parts of her dream had been a little sketchy, but the buildup had been explosive.

Pressing the cool glass to her forehead, she closed her eyes. If a dream could get her that worked up, what would the real thing be like?

She drank the last of the lemonade, put the glass in the sink and went out the back door, pulling on her gloves as she walked toward the old tree.

With the lower branches gone, it looked even more pathetic than it had before. It looked taller, too, she thought, gazing up. There was a stepladder in the garage that would allow her to reach the next three or four branches.

"No point in stopping now," she muttered, and set off toward the garage.

She was coming out of the garage, carrying the ladder, when Chay drove up.

Her heart seemed to skip a beat the moment she saw him.

With a wave of his hand, he parked in front of the porch and got out of the truck. "Hey, what's the ladder for?"

"I'm cutting down a tree in the back-yard."

"I don't believe it."

"Well, it's true!"

"Here, let me carry that," he said, relieving her of her burden.

"Thanks. I could have carried it, you know. I'm not helpless."

"I never said you were," Chay replied.

In spite of her words to the contrary, she was glad she didn't have to tote the heavy ladder. Made of wood, it was as tall as she was, and weighed almost as much.

Chay grunted softly when he saw the tree. "Were you planning to cut down the whole thing?" he asked, glancing at her over his shoulder.

"Hardly. I was just . . ." She shrugged. "Pruning it."

Laughing out loud, he put the ladder down next to the tree, then pulled a pair of leather gloves from his back pocket. Grabbing the saw, he climbed to the top of the ladder and began sawing the nearest branch.

Dana watched the play of muscles beneath his chambray shirt. Being a modern woman, she should have been offended that he had so high-handedly assumed that he could do the job better than she could.

Of course, it was hard to be offended when he was right. Then, too, letting him take over gave her a chance to watch him work, something that was extremely enjoyable.

Standing in the shade, she admired the way his jeans molded his tight buns and hugged the length of his long, long legs. She admired the width of his powerful shoulders, the ease with which he cut through a branch as thick as her thigh, the way his muscles bunched and relaxed as he tackled the next branch, and then all the ones within reach in the time it had taken her to saw through one.

She laughed softly. Sometimes it just took a man to do a man's job, and my oh my, but Chay was all man.

"What are you laughing at?" Chay asked, glancing down at her.

"Oh, nothing."

"Uh-huh. We need a taller ladder. I can climb up a little higher and get the next few branches, but —"

"Oh, I don't think that's a good idea!"

"Worried about me?" he asked with a wicked gleam in his eye.

"What if I am?"

"Just checking." Climbing down from the ladder, he studied the tree for a few moments. "I think maybe it would be easier to just cut the tree down and then chop it up for firewood."

"Why didn't you think of that sooner?"

His gaze moved over her, long and slow and hot. "I had other things on my mind," he said. "The way you were watching me nearly singed my back pockets."

"I wasn't watching you!"

"No?" he asked, a challenge in his eyes.

"Well, maybe a little," she admitted.

He lifted one eyebrow. "Just a little?"

"Oh, for goodness' sake, just cut down the tree."

"All in good time. We need to discuss my payment first."

"Payment! What kind of payment?"

"I'll think of something." His gaze lingered on her lips. "Let's see . . ." He counted the branches he had already cut. "Nine branches." He looked thoughtful for a moment. "How about a kiss for each branch? That sounds about right to me."

"You're kidding!" she exclaimed, but her stomach was already turning somersaults at the thought of his mouth on hers.

"Too much?" he asked, smothering a grin.

"Well, perhaps not."

"Okay," he said in a brisk, businesslike tone. "Nine kisses and one glass of lemonade."

She was laughing now.

The sound wrapped around Chay's heart. It was good to see her smile and hear her laughter. "So," he said, "do you want to pay up now?"

"Do you want to collect your pay all at once?"

He nodded. "I think so." He pulled her into his arms. "Remember, we still have to discuss the payment for cutting down the tree and chopping it into firewood."

"I'm not sure I can afford that."

"I'll go easy on you," he murmured as he drew her closer.

She swallowed hard. "Will you?" she asked breathlessly.

"Trust me," he said, and kissed her.

Liquid heat flowed through her veins as his mouth settled over hers in a long, drawn-out kiss.

He drew back, a mischievous look in his eyes. "That's one."

She blinked up at him. "I'm not sure I'll survive two."

"Sure you will, darlin'," he said. "Just hang on tight."

To her amazement, each kiss was a little different from the last. Where the first was long and slow, the second was as quick as a flash of lightning and charged with electricity. The third was a delicious dueling of tongues, the fourth, fifth and sixth were a series of quick butterfly kisses on the tip of her nose and her eyelids. After the seventh, she lost the ability to think. She was drowning in an ocean of sensation, her whole body aching and alive and yearning for more than kisses. Much more.

When he withdrew his lips from hers, it took her a moment to realize that he was no longer kissing her.

"Nine," he said.

She nodded.

"I think I should have asked for more."

Dana shook her head. One more kiss, and she would have been pulling him down on the grass and begging him to make love to her. And she didn't want that, wasn't ready for that. Was she?

"Hey." He chucked her under the chin. "You still owe me a glass of lemonade."

"What? Oh, yes, of course." Turning on her heel, she hurried toward the house. Space, that was what she needed.

But it wasn't to be. Chay followed her through the back door and into the kitchen, stood with his hip braced against the corner of the counter while she filled two glasses with ice and lemonade, then handed him one. She took a long drink, hoping to put out the fire that was still roaring through her. If his kisses could make her feel like this, what would making love to him be like?

Chapter Eight

The memory of Chay's kisses stayed with Dana long after Chay had gone home. Because he had work to do at the ranch, he had told her he would be back tomorrow to finish cutting down the tree, payment to be determined later.

The thought of what that payment might be kept her awake into the wee small hours of the morning and followed her into her dreams when she finally fell asleep, dreams that featured a tall, dusky-skinned man riding across the prairie on a big black horse. In her dream, he rescued her from a horrible fate — on waking, she couldn't remember what it was — then carried her away with him to a hide tepee pitched beside a bubbling brook where he took her into his arms and made love to her for hours and hours.

She woke to the touch of the sun on her face, expecting to find him lying there beside her.

She shook off her disappointment at waking in bed, alone.

"Geez, get a grip, Dana Elizabeth Westlake!" she muttered. "Have you already forgotten about Rick? No matter how sexy Chay Lone Elk might be, he's not for you, remember? You've sworn off men for life!"

But she couldn't stop thinking about him. Not through breakfast or while she was washing the dishes or in the shower or while she was throwing her dirty jeans into the washer. The worst part was, even though she kept telling herself to forget him, she didn't really want to.

He hadn't said what time he would be there today so, of course, no matter where she was or what she was doing, she kept going to the front window or the door, hoping for a sign of him.

It was just after lunchtime when he drove up.

As usual, butterflies erupted in her stomach at the mere sight of him. Today, he wore a pair of faded blue jeans and a plaid shirt with the sleeves rolled up to his elbows. She watched him slide out of the cab of the truck, her gaze drawn to him like the proverbial moth to a flame. And, like the moth, her fate would be sealed if she let him get too close. Reaching into the back of the truck, he pulled out a saw, not an old rusty handsaw like the one she had been using the day before, but a nice shiny new chain saw with a wicked-looking blade.

He held it up and grinned at her. "It's important to have the right tool for the right job."

"Looks dangerous."

He shrugged. "It can be." He drew on a pair of heavy work gloves. "That's why I'm going to be very, very careful."

She nodded. "Anything I can do?"

"Just stay out of the way," he said, putting on a pair of safety glasses.

"I can do that."

With a wink, he walked over to the tree and set to work. Soon the air was filled with the whine of the saw. Wood chips exploded through the air. A bird hopped from branch to branch and finally, with an angry screech, flew off in search of quieter lodgings.

It was while she was watching Chay cut through the trunk that she remembered they hadn't discussed what his payment would be.

Would he ask for more kisses? The mere thought made her heart race. Or would he ask for something else? Something more intimate than kisses? That thought sent a rush of heat to her cheeks. But of course he wouldn't ask for *that!* She told herself she was relieved and tried to make herself believe it.

Noting the way he was sweating while he worked, she went into the house to make a pitcher of fresh lemonade. She had made another apple pie the night before — because she happened to have a lot of apples, of course. She cut a large slice for Chay, a smaller one for herself, put the plates, two glasses filled with ice and the pitcher on a tray, and carried them outside, only then noticing the quiet. Was he finished already?

Rounding the corner of the house, she saw that he had stopped working and that he was no longer alone. Ashley had arrived and the two of them were so deep in conversation that neither of them noticed Dana's presence.

". . . and talk to him!" Ashley was saying. "He won't listen to me."

"You're only fifteen," Chay said.

Ashley straightened her shoulders and stuck out her chest, displaying an impressive amount of cleavage. "I'm almost sixteen!"

"A vast age, to be sure."

"Oh! I can't believe it! You're siding with him! I thought you'd be on *my* side." Ashley turned her back on Chay. Noticing Dana for the first time, she said, "You'd let me go on a double date, wouldn't you?"

"At fifteen? I don't think so."

"Why is it grown-ups always stick together?" Ashley exclaimed. She turned to face Chay again. "In the old days, women were having babies at my age. And I'll be sixteen next month!"

"They're still having babies at your age," Chay remarked dryly, "which is probably why your old man won't let you go out on a date."

Ashley sent a look at Chay that could have peeled paint off a wall, then, with a huff that clearly said she was fed up with the entire adult population, she jumped on the back of her horse and rode out of the yard.

Muttering something under his breath, Chay stared after her.

Dana set the tray on a crate, then handed Chay one of the glasses. "Here, you look like you need something to help you cool off."

"Thanks." He shook his head. "Kids. Why do they all want to grow up so fast?"

Dana picked up the other glass. "Didn't

you, when you were that age?"

"Yeah, I guess so. The thing is, Ashley and her old man don't get along and they can't talk to each other. They never could. A girl that age needs a mother, or at least a woman to look after her. All Ashley's got is the old man's housekeeper and she's so old, I'm sure she's forgotten what it was like to be young."

"It's never easy, is it?"

"No."

"Are you hungry?" she asked, gesturing at the tray.

Chay picked up one of the plates. "My favorite."

She shrugged. "It's no big deal. I had a lot of apples and I didn't want them to go to waste."

"Uh-huh." He wolfed down the pie, then smacked his lips appreciatively. "You know what they say, don't you? About the way to a man's heart?"

"Yeah, right."

"So," he asked, "what happened to all those huckleberries?"

She shrugged. "I decided to make jam out of them."

He grinned a knowing grin. "You made this apple pie because you know it's my favorite. Admit it."

"Maybe I did," she said, stifling a grin. "And maybe I didn't."

"You did," he said confidently. "You can't fool me."

Lifting the glass, he drained it in three long swallows. Setting it aside, he wrapped one long muscular arm around Dana's waist and drew her close.

"What are you doing?" she exclaimed.

"What do you think?" Lowering his head, he kissed her, long and deep. "I'm collecting part of my payment in advance."

"Oh."

He winked at her. "We'll talk about the balance later," he said with a roguish grin.

Replacing his safety glasses, he grabbed up the chain saw and went back to work.

Too nervous to sit still, Dana carried the tray back into the house. Standing at the sink, she washed the plates, her gaze constantly straying toward Chay. She had known him for less than two weeks. How had he become so important in such a short time? And how was she to know what she really felt for him? She knew very little about the man, yet he occupied practically every waking moment, and most of her sleeping ones!

Maybe it was just a case of good old-fashioned lust. After all, he was tall, dark and handsome and blessed with enough charisma for a dozen movie stars. It didn't hurt that he looked good sitting a horse or wearing a cowboy hat, or that he had a hard lean muscular body that beckoned her touch. She reminded herself that there was more to love than just physical attraction, that it took time to get to really know and care about someone, and that the only way to do that was to spend a lot of time together. And she didn't have a lot of time. In less than two weeks, she would be back at work in Ashton Falls, with no hope of any more time off until her vacation next year.

She washed the forks and glasses, then picked up a towel and began to dry the dishes. In a year, Chay Lone Elk would be nothing but a pleasant memory. But until then, she couldn't seem to stop watching him!

She watched appreciatively as he approached the back door. He rapped his knuckles on the wood, then stepped into the kitchen.

"All done?" she asked.

He pulled off his gloves and shoved them into the back pocket of his jeans. "Yep. Got any of that lemonade left?"

"Sure." She poured him a glass, watched

with something akin to fascination as he gulped it down, then dragged the back of his hand across his mouth.

"So," he said, "I'm thinking dinner and a movie on Friday night might just take care of the balance due."

"Is that right?"

"I'd like to make it sooner, but I'll be busy running the girls around until then. So, how does Friday night sound?" His gaze moved over her ever so slowly. "Of course, if that doesn't suit you, I could probably think of something else. Something a little more intimate." His gaze lingered on her lips. "You wouldn't even have to leave home."

"Pick me up at seven."

"Another hope crushed!" He grinned good-naturedly. "Seven it is." He handed her his empty glass. "See you then."

Thursday morning after breakfast, Dana went into town. As she walked down the street, window-shopping and pausing now and then to say hello to people she hadn't seen in years, she was surprised to find herself wondering what it would be like to live there. True, it wasn't a big city like Ashton Falls, but there was something to be said for living in a town where everyone knew you and you knew everyone. Even though she hadn't been in Wardman's Hollow for several years, people remembered her. Back home, she didn't even know her neighbors, and she had lived next to them for over three years. Walking down the streets at home, she never saw anyone she knew. At night, she made sure all the doors and windows in the house were locked.

She ate lunch at the café, then went to Wright's and picked up a few groceries. She took the long way home, admiring the beauty of the countryside. Back in Ashton Falls, there was little to see but look-alike houses and tall buildings with mirrored windows. Out here, cows and horses grazed in pastures on both sides of the road. There were trees and mountains, hay fields and haystacks, vacant lots dotted with wildflowers, men riding tractors, kids riding horses. The sky was a gorgeous blue, the air clean and filled with the scents of hay and grass instead of gray and smoggy. Once, she pulled off the road and spent ten minutes watching an eagle soar overhead.

She spent the rest of the day considering the pros and cons of moving to Wardman's Hollow. Of course, it all boiled down to

Chay Lone Elk. Did she want to give up her job and her life in Ashton Falls for a man she had met less than two weeks ago? Did she want to risk her heart again so soon? And what if nothing came of her attraction to him? Would she still want to live here?

She shook her head. Her life sounded like a soap opera. Will John come home? Will Mary find love again? Tune in next week, same time, same station.

Friday morning bloomed bright and clear. Dana's first thought on rising was that she had a date with Chay. He was in her thoughts constantly, whether she was changing the sheets on the bed or washing the breakfast dishes. She wondered what he was doing and if she was in his thoughts the way he was forever in hers.

She was thumbing through a fashion magazine she had picked up at the store when the phone rang.

"Hello?"

"Seven o'clock," said a deep male voice. "Don't forget."

Dana smiled. "I'll be ready."

"Can you be ready at six?" he asked. "I don't think I can wait until seven."

She smiled. "I can't wait, either, but

what about the girls?"

"Big John's home. The girls decided to stay in tonight. They're going to roast marshmallows in the fireplace and watch some DVDs. So, what have you been doing all day?"

"Thinking about you, mostly," she admitted.

"Really?" She heard the smile in his voice. "Well, darlin', I've been thinking about you, too." She heard voices in the background, then he said, "Listen, I've got to go."

"All right."

"See you soon."

"Bye." Smiling, she hung up the phone.

She was on pins and needles the rest of the day. At four, she took a long bubble bath, then washed and blow-dried her hair. By five-thirty, she had tried on every outfit she had brought with her at least twice. At five forty-five, she decided on a pink-and-white-print sundress and a pair of sandals. She ran a brush through her hair, applied a fresh coat of lipstick and managed to look calm and cool when he knocked on the door ten minutes later, even though her heart was beating a mile a minute.

As always, her breath caught in her throat at the sight of him. Tonight, he wore black jeans and a long-sleeved black shirt over a white T-shirt.

He whistled under his breath when he saw her. "Honey, you look good enough to eat."

"Thank you." She knew she was blushing but she couldn't help it. She knew the pink-and-white sundress she had chosen flattered both her figure and her complexion, but nobody had ever looked at her quite the way Chay was looking at her.

Taking her by the hand, he led her out of the house and down the stairs. He held the truck door open for her, then slid behind the wheel and gunned the engine to life.

"Where are we going?" she asked.

"I thought we'd go to the steak house, if that's okay with you."

She nodded. She wasn't much for red meat, but the steak house served a great Cobb salad and had some of the best sourdough bread she had ever eaten.

"How's Ashley doing?" she asked.

"I don't know. She and the old man got into it again just before I left. Seems like all they do is argue lately. Ashley locked herself in her room and wouldn't come out. The Three Musketeers are hiding out in the family room watching a movie. I tried to talk to Ashley, but she wasn't having any. And Big John . . ." Chay shook his head in disgust. "He doesn't give a rat's . . . sorry. I just wish he'd . . ."

Chay's voice trailed off when he saw the curiosity in Dana's eyes. His hand tightened on the wheel. He should tell her the truth, he thought, tell her the whole ugly thing, but why go into it? Dana would only be here for another week or so. What was the point in airing the old man's dirty laundry?

"Chay? Hey, where'd you go? One minute you're here, and the next you're a million miles away."

"What? Oh, sorry. Do you want me to come by tomorrow and cut that tree up for firewood?"

"Did I miss something?"

"What do you mean?"

"We were talking about Ashley and the trouble she's having with her father."

"Yeah, well, why don't we talk about something a little more cheerful?"

"Like what?"

"Practically anything. What do you like to do when you're not appraising antiques?"

"Oh, lots of things. Read. Jog. Go to the movies. What are we going to see tonight?"

"Whatever's playing," he said with a grin. "With only one theater in town, there's not a whole heck of a lot of choice."

"Right. I forgot."

Chay pulled into the restaurant parking lot a few minutes later. Inside, they were seated immediately.

Dana glanced around. "The place hasn't changed much since I was here last," she remarked. "Same tablecloths, same paper on the walls. Is the food still as good?"

"Best in town."

He looked up and smiled as the waitress came to take their order. In true manly fashion, he ordered a steak, rare, with all the trimmings, and a cup of coffee, black. She ordered the Cobb salad and a glass of iced tea.

They made small talk for a few minutes and then Chay started telling her about the ranch house he was building, describing it so beautifully that she could see it clearly in her mind, the big country kitchen, a living room with a big stone fireplace, a bedroom that faced the east, a front porch that faced the west so he could sit there in the evening and watch the sun set. "Of course, there's not much to see now," he said. "Just the foundation and a frame, but one of these days . . ."

"It sounds wonderful," she remarked. "I can't wait to see it . . ." Her voice trailed off. She would be long gone before his house was completed.

During dinner, she told him about some of the rare antique vases and furniture she had appraised. "I love the look and feel of old oak," she said. "It's so beautiful. In the old days, men took pride in their work, you know? You can almost see the love they put into each piece. You're laughing at me," she said when he grinned.

"No, not at all. It just seems, I don't know, odd to hear a pretty, young woman carrying on about antiques." He grinned at her. "I always thought appraisers were a bunch of old men who were almost as ancient as the pieces they appraised."

"Very funny."

He gestured at her plate. "You about done there? The show starts in fifteen minutes."

She nodded. "I'm through. And I'm stuffed."

"Good. I won't have to buy you any popcorn."

"No popcorn? Then I'm not going."

Grinning, he paid the check and they left the restaurant.

They reached the theater with five minutes to spare.

"Where do you like to sit?" Chay asked. "Front or back?"

"Either one."

"I like the back," he said. "Here's two together." The theater lights went off just as they sat down. Chay reached for her hand, his fingers threading through hers. The touch sent little frissons of pleasure moving through her.

The previews were still rolling when Chay's fingers tightened on her hand. "Is something wrong?" she whispered.

He swore softly. "Ashley's here."

"What? Where?" Dana peered into the darkness.

"Over there, on the aisle."

Leaning forward a little, Dana saw Ashley sitting beside a tall young man with long blond hair. "I thought you said she'd locked herself in her room?"

"Yeah. Dammit! What was she thinking?" He ran a hand through his hair. "If the old man finds out . . ."

"Relax," Dana whispered. "You can't do anything about it now."

"Yeah. Yeah, you're right." He settled back in his seat. A moment later, the movie began.

She didn't think Chay saw much of the movie. He spent most of the time watching Ashley. And Dana spent most of her time watching him and wondering why he was so concerned about his employer's teenage daughter. Not that that was a bad thing. She was glad he took his responsibility seriously. It was just that his worry seemed out of proportion, almost obsessive, somehow. He worried about Ashley as if she were a part of his family . . . but that was ridiculous. If Ashley were related to Chay, he would have told her so. Besides, they didn't act as if they were even remotely related.

With a shake of her head, Dana turned her attention back to the screen.

When the movie was over, Chay stood but didn't leave the theater. When Ashley and her boyfriend approached, Chay stepped out into the aisle, blocking their path.

"Chay!" Ashley's eyes grew wide. "What are *you* doing here?"

"I might ask you the same thing. Come on, let's get out of here."

"I'm going home with Nick."

Dana got her first good look at the boy beside Ashley. Blond and blue-eyed, he wore a cutoff sweatshirt and a pair of jeans with a hole in the knee. He had a gold hoop in one ear, and a tattoo of a spider spinning a web on his left shoulder. Dana thought he looked as if he was in his early twenties, far too old to be dating a girl on the shy side of sixteen.

She glanced at Ashley. She wore a bright pink tube top, a pair of skintight red jeans, lavender eye shadow and purple lipstick. Dana was shocked by the girl's appearance. Had she seen her on the street, she wasn't sure she would have recognized her. Always before, Ashley had been clean-scrubbed and well dressed.

"You're going home with me," Chay said. "Right now." He fixed the boy with a hard stare. "I don't want to see you around my . . ." Chay cleared his throat. "I don't want to see you with Ashley again, you got that?"

Nick nodded sullenly.

Taking Ashley by the hand, Chay turned and headed for the door, practically dragging her along behind him. Dana hurried after them.

Once they reached the parking lot, Chay rounded on Ashley. "What the hell were you thinking, going out dressed like that?" he demanded angrily. "Don't you care what people think?"

"How could you humiliate me like that?" Ashley replied heatedly.

"You should be humiliated, to be seen in public with that scumbag. What would your father say? Where'd you meet that loser, anyway?"

Ashley glared at him. "I met him at a party, if you must know. As for my dad, he doesn't even know I'm alive! I don't care what he thinks."

"Well, you'd damn well better care unless you want to spend the rest of your life locked in your room."

"You had no right to interfere like that," Ashley said hotly. "You're not my keeper!"

"No, but you sure need one."

"Everyone treats me like a child!"

"When we get back to the ranch, I'll tell the old man that Dana and I took you to the movies."

"Tell him the truth. I don't care!"

Chay blew out a breath of exasperation. "Listen, Ashley, I'm just trying to keep you out of trouble."

"Oh! You're just like my dad, always trying to keep me from having any fun," she muttered, and lapsed into a sullen silence.

"Dana, do you mind if I take you home first?"

"No, of course not."

They reached her place a short time later. Chay parked the truck, opened the door for her and walked her to the porch.

"I'm sorry," he said. "This isn't exactly the way I thought the evening would end."

"It's all right."

He drew her into his arms. "What are you doing tomorrow?"

Tomorrow! If Rick hadn't deserted her, it would have been her wedding day. "I . . . I think I'm just going to stay home."

He drew back a little. "I see."

"No," she said. "You don't."

"Then tell me."

How could she say it out loud?

"Come on, Dana, you can tell me anything. I don't want any secrets between us." He felt a little guilty as he said the last, since he was keeping several secrets from her.

"Tomorrow was supposed to be my wedding day."

He drew her back into his arms. "I'm sorry, honey. I guess there isn't much I can say to make things better."

She hid her face against his shoulder so he couldn't see her tears. He was right, there were no words to ease her pain, but it felt good to be in his arms, to hear his voice murmuring soft words of comfort. Did she dare trust her feelings for this man? Or was she just asking for another heartache? She had vowed never to love again, but she had been drawn to Chay from the first. Maybe it was fate. Maybe she was just on the rebound.

"Don't stay home alone tomorrow," he said, dropping a kiss on the crown of her head. "It's the old man's birthday tomorrow and he's giving himself a big party. Barbecue, rodeo, dancing, the whole nine yards. Say you'll come and cheer me on when I ride."

She had to admit it sounded a lot better than staying home alone, feeling sorry for herself. "You're going to ride in the rodeo?"

"You bet."

"Okay, I'll go," she said. "What time?"

He tapped her chin with his forefinger. "That's my girl. I'll pick you up around noon. The rodeo starts at one."

"What should I wear?"

"Jeans and a T-shirt are fine, but you might want to bring a dress along for later."

"All right."

He hugged her and then, no doubt mindful of Ashley watching them from inside the truck, he kissed her quickly. "Sweet dreams."

She murmured, "Good night," and then, as she had so often in the last few days, she stood on the porch and watched him drive away until he was out of sight.

Chapter Nine

Chay glanced at Ashley. She had moved as far away from him as she could get. She was staring out the passenger window, her arms folded across her chest.

"Is this the first time you've snuck out to meet that loser?" he asked.

"What difference does it make? It's none of your business, anyway."

"Did you look at yourself in the mirror before you left the house?"

"So you really don't like my outfit?"

"Not much. What look were you going for? Teenage hooker of the month?"

"Very funny. Don't you think I look sexy? Nick does."

"I think you look ridiculous."

She glared at him. "I do not."

"You don't see Dana parading around like that. What happened to Brandon? I thought you were stuck on him?"

She shrugged. "I like him okay, but

Nick's . . ." She lifted a hand and let it fall.

"Exciting?" Chay supplied dryly. "Forbidden?" He grunted softly, knowing he was on the right track by the look on her face. "You'd better hope we can sneak you into the house before Big John gets a look at the way you're dressed. If he says anything about your being gone, I'll tell him Dana and I took you to the movies with us."

"What makes you think he'll believe you? And what excuse will you give for not taking Megan and LuAnn and Brittany?"

"I don't know. I'll think of something."

"Even if he believes you, I'll still be in trouble," she said. "He'll yell at me for not telling him that I was going and then yell at me for going off with you when I had company."

"Like I said, I'll tell him it was just a misunderstanding, that I thought you'd told him, and that you thought I did. I'll tell him I asked the other girls and they didn't want to go. When we get home, you hightail it up to your room and wash that crap off your face, then get into bed. I'll talk to your old man."

"All right."

"Just promise me you won't pull a stunt like this again."

"I love Nick."

"Love! You don't even know what the word means. Besides, he's too old for you. Didn't you ever ask yourself why he isn't dating girls closer to his own age?"

"He loves me."

Chay swore under his breath. "How long have you known him?"

"Not very long," she admitted sullenly.

Chay took a deep breath. Anger and recriminations weren't the answer. "Listen, honey, you're gonna meet a lot of guys before you find the right one. But right now you need to be careful. There are a lot of guys out there who'll take advantage of you if they can. I don't want you to get hurt. Or to wind up pregnant."

"Is that all you're worried about? That I'll get pregnant?"

"I don't want you to get hurt, Ashley. I don't want to see you make a mistake that will ruin the rest of your life."

"Is that what you think babies do, ruin your life?"

"They do when you're fifteen and unmarried. Whether you keep it or give it away, you'll never be the same. Enjoy being young, Ashley. Don't get caught up in things you're not old enough to handle."

He pulled up alongside the house and cut the engine. "Get going."

He watched her shimmy up the tree that grew alongside the house and made a quick mental note to have one of the men cut off the big branch outside her window first thing in the morning.

Exiting the truck, he went into the house. He found Big John in the kitchen.

"Have you seen Ashley?" Big John asked. "She's been missing all night. Those silly girls said they didn't know where she was."

"She's fine. I took her to the movies."

"The movies! Why the hell didn't you tell me?"

"I thought she did."

"Well, she damn well didn't! I was just about to call the police. Where is she now?"

"Calm down. She's upstairs getting ready for bed."

"I'll be glad when she goes back to school."

"I'll miss you, too, Daddy."

Big John whirled around at the sound of his daughter's voice. Ashley stood in the doorway wearing a bathrobe over a pair of pajamas, her face scrubbed clean. Tears glistened in her eyes. Before Big John could say anything, she turned and ran down the hall.

Chay heard her footsteps running up the

stairs, the slam of a door.

Big John muttered something under his breath, then stalked out of the room.

Chay let out a heavy sigh, wondering if Ashley and the old man would ever find a way to get along. As far back as Chay could remember, the two of them had been at loggerheads. Big John had no patience for her, no time to spend with his only daughter.

Leaving the house, Chay determined that, in the future, he would keep a closer eye on Ashley's comings and goings whether she liked it or not.

Chapter Ten

It would have been her wedding day.

It was Dana's first thought when she woke on Saturday morning. Feeling thoroughly depressed, she stared up at the ceiling, overcome with a sense of lethargy. She never should have agreed to go to the barbecue with Chay today. She wasn't going to be good company for herself or anyone else. She hated feeling this way. She wasn't the first woman this had happened to and she wouldn't be the last. Why couldn't she just shake it off and get on with her life? It wasn't the end of the world.

She needed to call home. She had called her mother when she arrived at the Hollow, but that had been weeks ago. She had put off calling again because she didn't want to talk about Rick. Surprisingly, she had rarely thought of him at all, thanks to her infatuation with Chay.

She glanced out the window. It was a beautiful day. The words *happy is the bride the sun shines on* drifted through her mind. She wondered if it had been sunny on the day Rick married his new love. Rather uncharitably, she hoped there had been a cloudburst!

With a sigh, she grabbed a book and went into the bathroom where she took a long hot bubble bath. She didn't get out until the water was almost cold.

After dressing, she went downstairs and drank a glass of orange juice, then fixed herself a cup of strong black coffee.

She was stalling, but no matter how long she put it off, sooner or later she had to call her mother.

She felt a little better when she hung up thirty minutes later. Her mother, bless her heart, had taken care of everything, just as she'd said she would. She had called the guests, canceled the church and the flowers and the caterer, returned all the gifts. Friends and family had been sympathetic, her mother said, expressing their love and their regrets that things hadn't worked out.

Dana stared at the phone, thinking that she should just call Chay and tell him she couldn't make it. She was reaching for the phone when it rang. She knew, somehow, that it was him.

Lifting the receiver, she murmured a quiet hello.

"Good morning."

A familiar warmth filled her at the sound of his voice. "Good morning. I was just about to call you."

"I hope that means you were missing me as much as I was missing you," he said, and she heard the smile in his voice. "Any chance I could pick you up at eleven instead of noon?"

She opened her mouth, intending to tell him that she had changed her mind and that she wouldn't be going, but her heart had other ideas. "I'll be ready."

"Good. See you soon."

She hung up the receiver and glanced at the clock. Ten-fifteen! If she was going to be ready by eleven, she had to hurry!

Chay arrived at eleven on the dot. He was clad in a pair of faded blue jeans, a slipover buckskin shirt with fringe dangling from the sleeves and snakeskin boots. There was no mistaking his Indian heritage today.

"Hi, cowboy," she said, opening the door for him.

"Hey, gorgeous." He kissed her on the

cheek. "Are you ready?"

"Yes, just let me grab my bag." It was amazing, but just the thought of spending the day with him chased all the dark clouds from her mind. Who needed Rick when Chay was here?

She picked up her bag, which held a sweater in case it got cool, a dress and shoes for later, a brush, comb and her makeup.

Chay opened the truck door for her, winked at her, then went around to the driver's side and slid behind the wheel.

"Ready for a good time?" he asked.

She smiled at him. "More than ready. Thanks for asking me."

"Hey, I usually go to these things alone. Today I'll have the prettiest girl in town on my arm."

She blushed at the compliment. It wasn't true by any means, but she could have kissed him for saying it. Today, of all days, she needed to feel good about herself.

"So, you said Big John does this every year?"

"Yep. Guess he figures no one else could give him a party as big as the one he can throw for himself. It's something just about everybody in town turns out for."

"Amazing."

"Yeah, it is that."

"Do I sense a note of bitterness in your voice?"

"Probably."

She waited, but he didn't elaborate. "So," she said, "are you still baby-sitting?"

"No. Yesterday was the last day. Their folks are picking them up today. You don't know how relieved I am that they're going."

"Don't you like kids? They seemed like pretty nice girls to me."

"I love kids but four teenage girls are more than I can handle." He grinned at her. "I won't have to worry about them again until next summer. Who knows, the way girls grow up these days, they might all be married by then."

Dana nodded, her good mood momentarily shattered. Married. Today was to have been her wedding day.

"Hey," Chay said, taking her by the hand. "I'm sorry."

"It's okay."

He gave her hand a squeeze. "I was supposed to make you forget what day it is, not remind you."

"It's okay, really." She forced a smile, and changed the subject. "Will your mother be at the party? I'd like to meet her."

"I'd like for her to meet you, too. But it won't be today. I can't think of anything that would bring her back here."

"What about your father?" she asked.

A muscle worked in Chay's jaw, reminding her that his father was a topic that he had refused to discuss once before.

"I'm sorry," she said quickly. "Forget I asked." But she couldn't help wondering at Chay's reticence in talking about his father. Was it because his father wasn't Indian? Or, horrible thought, maybe he didn't know who his father was.

They pulled into the driveway of Big John's ranch a few minutes later. Chay parked alongside the house, switched off the ignition and stepped out of the truck. Walking around to the passenger side, he opened the door for Dana and handed her out of the cab.

She glanced around, awed by what she saw. A huge two-story white house sat on a small rise. A wide veranda stretched across the front. Dark green shutters hung at the windows upstairs and down. Tall trees grew along both sides of the house. Colorful flowers bordered a well-manicured lawn. There were cars and trucks parked everywhere. She guessed there were already close to fifty. Music filled the air, growing louder as Chay took her by the hand and led her around to the rear of the house.

Dana blinked at what she saw. There were men, women and children everywhere, most decked out in jeans, cowboy shirts, big hats and boots. There were four bounce houses for the kids, as well as a snow-cone machine and a cotton-candy machine. A man wandered around making balloon animals for the youngsters. A clown was entertaining old and young alike with a magic show. A couple of fiddlers stood off to one side playing country music.

A ways off in the distance, a group of men were throwing horseshoes. There was also a baseball game in progress. What looked like a whole side of beef was slowly turning over an open pit. Colorful canopies shaded two dozen long tables and another dozen round ones, all of which were laden with food. Galvanized tubs were filled with ice and every brand of beer and soft drink known to man. A large arena had been set up on one side, complete with bleachers.

Dana shook her head. "Wow."

Chay grinned at her. "Pretty impressive, huh?"

"I'll say. How many people is he expecting?"

"Oh, about two hundred, I guess, not counting kids. Do you want to get something to eat or drink?"

"Sure."

She had never seen such a spread in all her life. There were bowls of fresh fruits and vegetables, a variety of dips and sauces, trays of bread and rolls, cheeses, pickles and chips, salsa, barbecued chicken, Swedish meatballs and cocktail wieners, as well as hamburgers, hot dogs, shrimp cocktail and every kind of salad you could imagine, as well as carrot and celery sticks.

It all looked so good, Dana took a little of everything. "You gonna eat all that?" Chay asked incredulously.

"Just watch me," she replied, grinning.

He laughed out loud. "I like a girl with a healthy appetite. Come on, I see an empty table over there."

Sitting down, Dana took a good look at her plate and wondered if maybe she'd taken a bit more than she needed.

Chay put his plate on the table. "Best save some room," he warned. "This is just a snack."

"A snack?" she said in disbelief. "You

mean there's going to be more?"

"Sure. Dinner will be served after the rodeo."

The food was excellent and she ate way too much, considering there was more to come. She was looking forward to sitting in the shade, relaxing, when Chay stood and took her hand.

"Come on," he urged. "It's rodeo time."

"Already?"

"Yep."

He led her to the arena and found her a seat in front. "How about a kiss for luck?" He didn't wait for an answer, but swooped down and kissed her.

"Be careful," she admonished.

"Always," he said, winking at her.

Before long, the bleachers were full. Dana was feeling a little out of place until Ashley and her friends dropped down beside her.

"Hi."

"Hi, yourself," Dana replied, glad for the company. "Nice to see you again, girls."

LuAnn, Megan and Brittany grinned at her as they sat down.

"I love to watch Chay ride," Ashley said, munching on a hot dog. "He's the best."

"I've never been to a rodeo before," Dana said.

"Never?" Ashley looked at her as if she had just admitted she had never seen a horse before.

"I'm a city girl, remember?"

"You'll love it," LuAnn said.

Ashley grinned. "Chay wins every year, you know."

" 'Cause he's the best." The words were spoken simultaneously by Megan, Brittany and LuAnn. The way they said it led Dana to believe that the girls had heard the same thing from Ashley many times before.

"Well, he is!" Ashley said.

Just then the loudspeaker rumbled to life. "Afternoon, ladies and gents, kids of all ages. Welcome to Big John's birthday bash and rodeo. I sure hope you're ready for some excitement 'cause we've got some top broncs this year and they promise to give our cowboys a run for their money. The rider who scores the most points this year will win a cash prize of two thousand dollars and one of Big John's prize heifers. First up is saddle bronc riding . . ."

What followed was unlike anything Dana had ever seen before as one cowboy after another exploded out of the chute on the back of a thousand pounds of bucking horseflesh. It was the most amazing thing to watch and she was caught up in it until

162

she heard the announcer call Chay's name. Suddenly, what had been fun and exciting took on a whole new dimension. It had been one thing to watch strangers get thrown, but she knew Chay Lone Elk personally and that made all the difference in the world.

She leaned forward, hardly daring to breathe, as the chute opened and a big black horse came out bucking for all it was worth.

Ashley stood up, screaming, "Go, Chay! Yeah, Chay!" She looked down at Dana. "Isn't he great?"

"Great," she murmured, unable to take her gaze from Chay. He stuck to the saddle like glue, one arm raised over his head, his body rocking back and forth as the horse bucked and pitched. After what seemed like eight years but was only eight seconds, the whistle blew and the pickup man rode up alongside Chay.

Dana blew out a deep breath, relieved that it was over. Only it wasn't. Next came bareback bronc riding, then calf roping, then steer wrestling and then bull riding. Dana thought each event was worse than the last. Riding a bucking horse was bad enough, but then Chay came out on a bull that looked madder than hell and must have weighed two thousand pounds. And he won every event but steer wrestling, where he came in second.

Ashley yelled and screamed when they announced Chay had won the top prize of the day and Dana stood beside her, yelling until her throat hurt. For all that she had been scared to death the whole time, watching Chay ride had been the most exciting thing she had ever seen.

Moments later, he was taking a victory ride around the arena. Dana felt her heart turn over in her chest as she watched him wave to the crowd and then he was riding toward her.

Dismounting, he ducked under the bars of the corral and scooped her into his arms. The shouts and cheers of the crowd faded into the distance as he lowered his head and kissed her.

Dana felt her cheeks grow hot when the announcer said, "You can come up for air now, cowboy. Eight seconds has come and gone."

The crowd roared with laughter.

Chay kissed her again, then left to get cleaned up and change clothes for the barbecue.

Ashley linked her arm with Dana's. "Come on, let's go find a table." She glanced at her friends. "You coming?"

"No," LuAnn said. "We'll catch up with you later. Megan has to go eat with her parents and I told Brittany I'd help her watch her little sister while her mom nurses the baby."

"All right," Ashley said. "See ya."

The air was redolent with the scent of barbecued beef. The tables had been cleared of leftovers and now groaned under the weight of sliced beef, platters of corn on the cob and bowls of potato and macaroni salads, baked beans and baked potatoes, an assortment of rolls and bread and green salads.

Chay joined them a short time later. Taking her by one hand and Ashley by the other, he led the way to the front of the food line. "Winners always eat first," he told Dana with a wink.

Dinner was a lively, noisy affair. The air was filled with conversation and laughter. Dana laughed along with the other women at the table as Chay exchanged stories with the cowboys sitting on either side of him. They talked about bad broncs and rank bulls, about hauling hay in the middle of winter and breaking through ice to get water. They made jokes about being stomped and gored and snake-bit, about stampedes and breech births and why any man with any brains would work with cattle, surely the dumbest creatures on God's green earth.

"I don't know who's dumber," one of the women said, grinning, "the cows or the women who love the cowboys."

At that, one of the men started singing "Mama, Don't Let Your Babies Grow Up to Be Cowboys," then yelled "Ouch!" when his wife punched him on the arm.

After most everyone had gone back for seconds, or thirds, things quieted down a bit.

And then, as a man picked up a microphone and climbed up on a chair, the crowd broke into a round of applause.

Dana looked at Chay.

"That's Big John," Chay said. "He's about to make his yearly speech."

Dana studied the man. Big was an apt description, she thought. He was well over six feet tall, with a shock of dark brown hair, bushy brown eyebrows, a nose that had been broken at least once and a strong, determined jaw. Like most everyone else, he wore jeans, a plaid cowboy shirt, boots that probably cost more than her apartment and a Stetson.

"Welcome, friends and neighbors."

His voice was big, too, she thought.

"I hope you're all having a good time, and that you got enough to eat!"

Whistles, applause and shouts of affirmation rang out from the crowd.

"I'm glad to hear it!" Big John exclaimed. " 'Cause if you're still hungry, it sure as hell isn't my fault!"

Someone called, "Forget the sweet talk, you old horse thief, and tell us how old you are."

"It's a running joke," Chay told Dana. "Every year, people try to find out Big John's age."

"What's the big secret?" she asked.

Chay shrugged. "Beats the heck out of me."

"Do you know?"

"I've got a pretty good idea," Chay replied with a shrug.

A pretty, blond woman wearing a bright red, low-cut sundress sashayed up beside Big John and took the microphone from his hand. She nodded to the band and they broke into a rousing rendition of "Happy Birthday." The crowd began singing as two men came forward carrying the biggest cake Dana had ever seen.

Wearing a grin as wide as the Grand Canyon, Big John blew out the candles.

"Hey, John," called a man in a big black hat, "what did you wish for?"

"None of your business!" Big John hollered back, and then he looked at the lady in the red dress and waggled his eyebrows.

"That's a mighty young heifer you've got there," Black Hat said. "You sure you can handle her?"

"Damn right!" Big John said and, sweeping the blonde into his arms, he kissed her soundly.

The men in the crowd hooted and hollered.

Big John came up grinning. "I've had my dessert," he said. "You all help yourselves to yours. The dancing will start in about thirty minutes. Ladies, feel free to change into your dancin' duds up at the house." He slipped his arm around the blonde's waist. "You all have a good time now, hear? Oh, we've got plenty of guest rooms if any of you get so soused you don't want to drive home."

This announcement was met with more applause.

"I'm gonna go get some cake," Ashley said. "Do you guys want some?"

"Yes, thanks," Dana said.

Chay shook his head. "Bring me a beer, will you?"

"Okay." Rising, Ashley headed for the cake table.

A moment later, Big John made his way toward their table with the blonde hanging on his arm. "Evenin', Chay."

"John."

"Who's this pretty little filly?"

"Big John, this is Dana Westlake. Dana, this is Big John."

"Happy birthday," Dana said. Big John smiled at her. "Westlake? You're not related to Elsa, are you?"

"She was my grandmother."

"Wonderful woman. We were sorry to lose her."

"Thank you."

"How are your parents? I haven't seen them since they were up here, oh, when was it? Last year, I think."

"They're doing well, thank you."

Big John nodded. "Enjoy yourselves."

"Thank you."

She watched Big John walk away, then glanced at Chay. "You really don't like him, do you?"

"Not much."

"I think I'd quit if I were you. Why work for someone you don't like if you don't have to?"

He shrugged. "I don't know. Guess I'm

just a sucker for punishment."

Dana stared at him a moment, then frowned. Chay didn't look anything like Big John and yet there was something . . . before she could put her finger on it, Ashley returned carrying two enormous pieces of cake and a bottle of beer.

She set the plates on the table, handed the bottle to Chay, then plopped into her chair.

"What's wrong?" Dana asked.

"Everything."

Chay took a swig of beer. "What's bothering you now?"

"I'm bored." She glared at him. "If it wasn't for you, Nick would be here tonight."

"I don't want to go into that again," Chay said.

"Of course you don't. My life is ruined, but why should you care?"

Chay glanced past Ashley. "Cheer up. Here comes Brandon."

Ashley rolled her eyes. "Brandon! He's about as exciting as vanilla ice cream."

"Hey, Ashley," Brandon said, coming up behind her. "Are you going to the dance? Hi, Chay."

Ashley blew out a sigh. "Of course I'm going."

Chay glared at Ashley, warning her to mind her manners before saying, "Dana, this is Brandon DeHaven. Brandon, this is Miss Westlake."

"Pleased to meet you, Miss Westlake."

"Thank you, Brandon."

"Come on, Bran," Ashley said, rising. "Let's go find the girls."

Dana stared after the young couple as they disappeared into the crowd. "I thought she liked him."

"I thought so, too, but that was before she met Nick."

"Ah, yes," Dana said. "Nick, the bad boy. Why is it young girls are always attracted to boys like that?"

Chay shook his head. "You tell me."

"I was asking you."

"Beats the hell out of me. All I know is that Nick is trouble and she's chasing after it with both hands."

Dana had been inside nice homes before but Big John's house was unlike anything she had ever seen. The rooms were huge, the furniture comfortable and obviously expensive, as were the paintings on the walls and the sculptures on the shelves.

A maid escorted Dana to a guest room. "Just ring if you need anything," she said before closing the door.

Decorated in shades of hunter green and mauve, the room was quite lovely, with a king-size bed, a full-length mirror and a bathroom with a sunken tub.

Dana washed her hands and face, applied fresh makeup, then changed into the dress she had brought with her. Slipping on her sandals, she studied her reflection in the mirror. The dress complemented the color of her hair and skin, but she knew it was the prospect of dancing with Chay that had put the glow in her eyes and the flush in her cheeks. How had he become so important to her so fast? She was perilously close to losing her heart to a man she had met less than three weeks ago, a man she was afraid was keeping a secret from her. Though he had told her about his mother, she was certain that he was keeping something from her, but what? She hoped she was wrong.

She ran a brush through her hair, then left the room.

Chay was waiting for her at the foot of the stairs. He had changed clothes, too, and now he wore a pair of black jeans, a long-sleeved white shirt, a black leather vest and black boots. He looked good enough to eat.

The dance was held outside under a huge canopy. A six-piece band was playing a slow country tune when they arrived. The long tables had been taken down and a bar had been set up. Four bartenders handed out drinks and jokes. Colored lights ringed the dance floor. Several dozen couples were dancing while other guests conversed in small groups or stood at the bar, talking and laughing.

Chay nodded at the dance floor. "Shall we?"

She nodded and he led her onto the floor, then drew her into his arms. She nestled against him, her head resting on his shoulder. It felt wonderful to be in his arms, to feel his body brushing against hers, his breath warm upon her cheek. She felt cherished, protected, in a way she never had been before. It was a good feeling.

Sensing his gaze, she looked up, her eyes meeting his. Neither spoke. For a moment, her breath caught in her throat and then he was lowering his head toward hers. She closed her eyes, a sigh escaping her lips, her stomach fluttering in anticipation of his kiss, a kiss that was pure and sweet and achingly sensual all at the same time. A kiss that made her pulse race and her knees weak. His arm tightened around her waist and she grinned inwardly, wondering if it was passion that caused him to hold her closer or if he knew the effect his kiss was having on her and he was trying to keep her on her feet.

Gradually, she became aware that the music had stopped. Opening her eyes, she blinked up at Chay. He was grinning at her. At first, she didn't know why, and then she realized they were surrounded by couples, all of whom were watching them with varied expressions of amusement.

She felt a rush of heat climb up her neck into her cheeks when she noticed that Big John and the blonde in the red dress were standing nearby.

"You two better find a room or set a date," Big John suggested, his voice booming in the sudden stillness.

Dana felt her blush deepen.

Chay glowered at the older man. Taking Dana by the hand, he led her off the dance floor and into the shadows beyond.

"He's a fine one to talk," Chay muttered.

"What do you mean?"

"Nothing."

"You're doing it again," Dana said.

"Doing what?"

"You're muttering under your breath

about Big John. Honestly, I don't know why you work for the man. You're a top hand. I'm sure you could find another job."

"Yeah, I'm sure I could."

"So, why do you stay?"

"Maybe I'll tell you someday."

"But not tonight?"

"Not tonight." He blew out a deep breath, then drew her purposefully into his arms. "I can think of a lot of things I'd rather do than talk about that bullheaded old man," he said, and kissed her.

There was nothing remotely gentle about this kiss. It was bold and possessive and it drove every thought from her mind but her need to be held in his arms, to feel his lips on hers.

When he drew away, she knew she was lost. In spite of everything, she was falling in love with Chay Lone Elk.

Chapter Eleven

A loud pounding on the front door woke Dana from a sound sleep. Reaching for the lamp beside her bed, she turned on the light, grabbed her robe and hurried through the dark house to the door.

She peeked through the curtain that covered the front window, then quickly unlocked the door.

"Chay! It's after three o'clock. What are you doing here? Is something wrong?" A silly question, she thought. He wouldn't be there at such an hour unless something was wrong.

"Have you seen Ashley?"

"Not since the party. Why?"

"She's gone."

"Gone?" She stepped back. "Come in."

He followed her into the living room. Removing his hat, he ran a hand through his hair. "It looks like she's run away. I didn't think she'd come here, but I had to make sure."

"Why do you think she's run away?"

"Her bed hasn't been slept in. The old man called the girls. None of them has heard from her since they left the ranch last night."

"But why would she run away?"

"She had another fight with Big John. Apparently he caught her making out with Nick behind one of the barns." Muttering an oath, Chay removed his hat and ran a hand through his hair. "Dammit, I didn't even know Nick was at the party. I should have kept a better eye on her."

"Are you supposed to chaperon her all the time?" Dana asked. "I thought you only had to do that when she was away from the ranch."

"I'm responsible for her."

"Why?"

"Because the old man doesn't give a damn what she does most of the time." He jammed his hat back on his head. "I've got to go. I'm not going to find her hanging around here."

"Do you think she ran away with Nick?"

"If she did, I'll kill the little weasel. I told him to stay away from her."

Dana nodded. Looking at Chay, she felt a sudden fear for Nick. "Do you want me to go with you?" she asked, thinking she might be able to calm Chay down if they found Ashley and the young man together.

"Sure, if you want."

"Just give me a minute to get dressed." Going into her bedroom, she pulled on a pair of jeans and a long-sleeved sweater.

Chay was pacing the floor when she returned to the living room. Moments later, they were in the truck heading toward town.

"Do you know where Nick lives?" Dana asked.

"Yeah. He's got a room over one of the bars on Main Street."

"You seem to know a lot about him."

"Everybody knows about him. He's the town bad boy."

"What if she's not with him?"

"I hope to hell she isn't, but it's the only place I can think of that she might go."

"Does she stay in touch with her mother?"

"Sure. Jillian writes to her once a month or so. Jillian remarried a couple of years ago, some guy who sells RVs in Salt Lake."

"Would Ashley go there?"

"I don't know. She might."

A short time later Chay pulled over and parked in front of a rather seedy-looking saloon called the Dirty Shame.

Chay opened the door for her; then, hand in hand, they walked around the corner of the building to a flight of rickety wooden stairs. When they reached the top, Chay knocked on the door. If Nick was home, he would know, from that knock, that it wasn't a friend coming to call.

A couple of minutes passed before Nick opened the door. A cigarette dangled from a corner of his mouth, his hair was uncombed, he was shirtless and barefoot.

Looking over Nick's shoulder, Dana saw a girl sitting on a sofa. It was easy to see that they had recently made love.

Nick braced a shoulder against the doorjamb. "Yeah, what do *you* want?"

"I'm looking for Ashley."

"She ain't here."

"I can see that," Chay said brusquely. "Do you know where she is?"

"She called a few hours ago. Sounded like she was cryin'. She asked me to drive her to the airport. Said she was gonna go see her old lady."

"And you took her?"

"Hey, she wanted to go. What was I supposed to do?"

"Do you know what time her flight was leaving?"

Nick shrugged. "I don't know. Six, six-thirty."

"And you left her at the airport, alone?"

Nick took a step backward, obviously threatened by the menacing tone in Chay's voice.

"She said she was gonna get a room at the hotel across the street."

Chay clenched his hands into fists. For a moment Dana thought he was going to give Nick a much-needed punch in the nose. Instead, he turned away from the door. Dana followed him down the stairs.

"Looks like you called it," Chay said when they were back inside the truck.

"Lucky guess. Now what?"

"I'm going after her." He started the engine and pulled away from the curb. "Do you want to go along?"

"Sure."

"If we don't get there in time to stop her, I'll be going on to Salt Lake."

Dana smiled. "Sounds like this might turn into quite an adventure."

"Yeah," he said dryly. "An adventure."

They drove in silence for a time. Dana looked out the window, her mind on Ashley. It amazed her that the girl had the nerve to run away in the middle of the night and ask Nick to take her to the airport.

She slid a glance at Chay. He was watching the road, both hands clenched on the wheel. She wondered again at his devotion to Ashley Wardman, especially in view of his obvious dislike for Ashley's father. While she found it odd, she also found it strangely appealing that Chay was so concerned for Ashley's welfare. It boded well for the kind of father he would be when he had children of his own . . . beautiful children, no doubt, with dusky skin and black hair.

She couldn't help but envy the woman who would give him those children. . . . She shook the thought aside, annoyed by the surge of jealousy that rushed through her at the thought of Chay holding another woman, kissing her, making love to her. Again, she wondered how she had come to care so much in such a short time, and what she would do when it was time to go back home.

"I would never have had the nerve to run away like this when I was Ashley's age," Dana remarked.

"She's not afraid of much," Chay replied. "She goes to see her mother a couple times a year, so she's used to flying and she knows how to make reservations."

"Where did she get the money?"

Chay grunted softly. "She's got more money in the bank than a lot of men I know, including me. The old man's always giving her cash. He gives her money when she gets good grades and money when he misses a school event, which is most of them. He gives her money for her birthday and Christmas and whenever his conscience starts to bother him. The sad thing is, she'd rather have his attention than the money."

Dana nodded. All girls wanted and needed their father's attention and approval.

Bright lights signaled they were approaching the airport. Chay parked the truck. Minutes later, they were checking departure flights to Salt Lake City. There was a flight at 6:05. The next flight was at one o'clock in the afternoon.

Dana checked her watch. It was a quarter after five.

"Let's go," Chay said. "If we hurry, we should be able to catch her."

As luck would have it, the passengers hadn't boarded yet.

Chay spotted Ashley immediately and struck out in her direction.

The girl didn't look at all happy, Dana thought as she hurried after Chay. Ashley was sitting in a corner by herself, her arms crossed over her chest, looking as lost and alone as only a teenage girl can.

Ashley looked up, obviously startled to see Chay standing in front of her.

In the next instant, the little-girl-lost evaporated, to be replaced by a look of bored indifference. "What are you doing here?"

"Taking you back home where you belong."

Ashley shook her head. "I'm going to see my mom."

"If you wanted to worry the old man, you've done it. He had some kind of attack when he found out you were missing."

Ashley made a sound of mingled disgust and disbelief.

"It's true," Chay insisted. "The doc was at the ranch when I left or I'd have been here sooner."

Dana looked at Chay in surprise. Why hadn't he told her that? What other secrets was he keeping from her? Of course, it wasn't really a secret, but why hadn't he told her? Why was he so reluctant to share things with her?

"Why didn't you tell me?" Dana asked.

He shrugged. "I was worried about finding Ashley. Nothing else seemed important."

"Is he going to be all right?" Ashley asked anxiously.

"Sure. He's too mean to die." Chay held out his hand. "Come on, let's go."

Ashley hesitated a moment, then put her hand in Chay's and let him pull her to her feet.

"Do you have any luggage?"

"Just my carry-on."

He picked up her bag and they headed for the exit, the silence between them thick enough to cut with a knife.

When they reached the truck, Chay tossed Ashley's bag into the back, then unlocked the doors. Dana got in first and Ashley climbed in after her. Chay shut the door behind them; a little harder than Dana thought was necessary.

Sliding behind the wheel, he put the key in the ignition and pulled out of the parking lot.

Dana sat between the two of them. The tension in the cab was so thick, it fairly crackled. Ashley stared out the window, her whole body rigid, anger radiating off her like heat from a forest fire. Chay had a stranglehold on the wheel.

"Why'd you run away?" he asked at length.

Ashley didn't answer, only continued to

stare out the window. Just when Dana was sure she wasn't going to reply, Ashley said, "I wanted to be with someone who has time for me. Someone who'll listen to me. Someone who loves me."

"I love you," Chay said quietly.

Ashley turned away from the window and looked at him. "Do you, Chay?" she asked, and Dana heard the hopeful note in the girl's voice.

"Of course I do," Chay said. "Like a brother."

"You've always been there for me, just like a big brother, and I love you for it, but . . . I wanted to be with my mom, with family that loves me."

"The old man's your family and he loves you," Chay said.

"No, he doesn't!" Ashley retorted, her eyes flashing. "He's not worried about me. All he cares about is what people think. He wants everyone to believe he's the perfect father. Well, he's not! He's mean and —"

"Don't say something you'll regret later," Chay warned.

The fire went out of Ashley. Shoulders hunched, she stared out the window again.

After a time, the silence got to Dana and she turned on the radio, flipping through the stations until she found one playing country music.

They were nearing town when Chay said, "Do you mind if I drop Ashley off before I take you home? It might do the old man some good to know she's all right."

"I don't mind."

A short time later, Chay pulled up in front of the Wardman ranch house. Ashley got out of the truck and ran up the stairs and into the house.

Chay let out a sigh. "I'm tired and I'm hungry," he said. "Do you want to come in and have some breakfast before I take you home?"

He looked tired, she thought. There were dark shadows under his eyes and he looked just plain beat. She was pretty sure most of it came from worrying about Ashley. "Sounds good."

She followed him up the porch steps and into the house, which was eerily silent.

Chay removed his hat and hung it on the rack inside the front door. He glanced up at the second floor, wondering how Big John was doing. Wondering why he cared.

"Come on," he said, and she followed him down a long narrow hallway into a spacious kitchen.

There was a woman standing at the

stove. She was short and plump with a knot of gray hair. She turned when they entered the room. A broad smile lit her face when she saw Chay.

" 'Mornin', Mr. Chay. Can I fix you and your friend some breakfast?"

"Sounds good, Anna Mae," he said. "Dana, this is Anna Mae Waters, the best cook this side of the Mississippi. Anna Mae, this is Dana Westlake."

"Pleased to meet you, Anna Mae," Dana said.

"Why, it's right nice to meet you, too, Miss Westlake. What can I fix for you?"

Dana lifted her hand and let it fall. "Oh, I don't know. Anything is fine with me, really."

"I'll have pancakes and bacon," Chay said. "And a cup of black coffee."

"I'll bet you want that coffee now," Anna Mae said.

"You're an angel."

She beamed at him. "Coming right up. Pancakes and bacon all right with you, Miss Westlake?"

"Sure."

"All right, skedaddle," Anna Mae said, making a shooing motion with her hands. "You know I don't like anybody in my kitchen when I'm cooking."

With a grin, Chay held the door open for Dana, then followed her into the dining room.

He gestured at a chair covered in a deep wine-colored velvet. "Make yourself at home."

They had no sooner sat down than Anna Mae came in carrying a coffeepot and two large mugs. She poured them each a cup, then looked at Dana. "Do you take cream and sugar?"

"No, black is fine."

With a nod, Anna Mae returned to the kitchen.

Dana picked up her mug and took a sip. It was, she thought, the best coffee she had ever tasted.

She studied Chay over the rim of her cup. She noticed again how tired he looked, but what she saw was more than just weariness. Worry took a heavy toll on a man, she thought as she glanced around the room. Like the rest of the house, it was lavishly appointed. The table at which she sat probably cost more than her whole house and everything in it. Twelve chairs ringed the table. There was a matching breakfront filled with crystal and silver. A painting of a buffalo stampede hung on one wall.

She wondered if all of Big John's hired hands were welcome in the house and if Anna Mae cooked breakfast for them, too. Sometimes it seemed like Chay was almost part of the family.

She stared at Chay. She had been wondering for days who Chay reminded her of and now she knew. It was Big John. There was nothing as obvious as the two of them having the same color hair or build, but they had the same eyes, the same strong stubborn chin, the same way of walking, as though they owned the world and everything in it.

The thought had no sooner crossed her mind than she remembered thinking that Ashley bore a strong resemblance to Chay. . . .

"Why are you looking at me like that?" Chay asked, frowning.

She shook her head. "No reason."

Before he could question her further, Anna Mae entered the room carrying a large covered tray. In moments, a feast was spread before them: golden-brown pancakes dripping butter, strips of lean perfectly cooked bacon, fluffy scrambled eggs, bran muffins warm from the oven and a pitcher of fresh-squeezed orange juice.

Dana shook her head. "Is this just for

189

the two of us?" she asked Chay when Anna Mae left the room, "or are you expecting company like, say, the whole town?"

Chay forked three pancakes onto his plate. "Anna Mae believes breakfast is the most important meal of the day."

"It looks to me like she thinks it's the *only* meal of the day."

Chay grinned at her, then filled his plate with bacon and eggs. "Best dig in before it's gone."

Dana helped herself to a couple of pancakes, a strip of bacon and a spoonful of eggs.

"Is that all you're gonna eat?" Chay asked. "You'll hurt Anna Mae's feelings."

"Well, I wouldn't want to do that." Dana picked up a bran muffin and cut it in half. She slathered it with butter and took a bite. It was so light, it practically melted in her mouth. The rest of the food was just as good, everything cooked and seasoned to perfection.

"No wonder you don't want to leave here," Dana remarked.

She glanced upward, her attention drawn by the sound of Ashley's voice.

". . . see him anytime I want and if you don't like it, well, I just don't care!" The girl's voice rose with every word. A door

190

slammed and then Dana heard the sound of feet running down the stairs.

A moment later, Ashley burst into the room, her eyes red and swollen. She looked at Dana, then threw herself in Chay's arms. "He's so mean! Why won't he let me go to Mom's? He won't even know I'm gone!"

Chay stroked Ashley's back. "You're his daughter," he said quietly. "He may not know how to show you that he loves you, but he does."

"Oh, stop defending him. You don't like him and everybody knows it!"

"No, I don't, but that doesn't matter. He's your father, and you should respect him."

"That's easy for you to say. He's not your father."

A muscle worked in Chay's jaw.

"I wish *you* were my father!" Ashley said. "At least you listen to me. You don't treat me like I'm six years old. Well, you do sometimes, but you never —"

"Your father!" Chay exclaimed, cutting her off. "Hell, it's hard enough being your brother. . . ."

Chay closed his mouth with a snap, and silence fell over the room.

Ashley jumped to her feet. "What did you say?"

Chay looked up at her, his hands clenched in his lap. "Nothing."

"Brother." Ashley drew the word out, as if she had never heard it before. "You're my brother?"

Chay blew out a heavy sigh that seemed to come from the soles of his feet. "Yeah."

"I don't believe you. Why didn't you tell me before? Why didn't anyone tell me?"

"Big John made me swear not to tell anyone."

"But why?" Ashley asked, her eyes wide with disbelief.

"Why? Because he didn't want anyone to know he had a half-breed bastard for a son, that's why."

"I don't believe you."

"It's true whether you believe it or not."

"All this time, and you never told me." She shook her head. "How could you keep a secret like that? How could he?" She stared at Chay. "I've got a brother. I don't know whether to laugh or cry."

Chay pushed his chair away from the table. Rising, he drew Ashley into his arms. "I wanted to tell you," he said quietly. "You don't know how many times I started to tell you."

She rested her head on his shoulder. "I

wish you had. It sure explains a lot," she said wryly.

Chay grinned. "Yeah, I guess it does."

"Do we have any other brothers or sisters that I don't know about?"

"I hope not."

Ashley looked up at Chay. "Can't you talk to him for me, please? I want to go stay with my mom. I need to be with her for a while, you know? Sometimes a girl needs her mother."

"I know, but I don't think the old man will listen to anything I've got to say. He never has. And this really isn't a good time to upset him."

Ashley sighed dramatically. "Yeah, I guess you're right. But you'll talk to him, won't you? As soon as he's better?"

"Sure."

"Thanks, big brother." She kissed him on the cheek, then left the room.

Chay watched her out of sight, then sat down at the table again. He frowned when he saw the expression on Dana's face.

"Are you hiding any other secrets?" she asked, her tone icy. "You don't have a wife and six kids somewhere, do you?"

A muscle worked in Chay's jaw. "Of course not. You heard what I told Ashley. I promised Big John I wouldn't tell anyone.

Anyone," he repeated. "That includes you." He took a deep breath. "I wanted to tell you, just like I wanted to tell Ashley, but a promise is a promise."

"Yes," Dana said slowly. "I suppose so."

"But you think I should have told you anyway?"

"Yes. No. I don't know." She pushed away from the table and stood up. "It's been a long night. I'd like to go home."

With a nod, Chay rose from the table.

She couldn't think of anything to say on the ride home. Apparently, neither could Chay. Dana stared out the window, annoyed with herself for being angry with him. He was right, a promise was a promise and yet, right or wrong, she felt as though he had lied to her. Maybe it didn't matter that Big John was his father and Ashley was his sister. Maybe she was making a mountain out of a molehill, but it hadn't been that long ago that another man had lied to her. She didn't believe for a minute that Rick had fallen head over heels in love with the blond bombshell in a matter of days. Looking back, Dana was certain he had been dating his secretary while he was engaged to her. Now that she thought of it, there had been too many times when he had canceled a date at the last minute, or made some flimsy excuse to take her home early. Once she had caught the scent of perfume on him that wasn't hers. When questioned, Rick had said a saleslady spritzed him with perfume by mistake. How could she have been so blind!

Lost in thought, she didn't realize they had reached her house until Chay pulled up in front of the porch.

"Thanks for bringing me home." She reached for the door handle, hoping he would say something, anything, to stop her.

But he just looked at her, his dark eyes giving nothing away.

Fighting back her tears, she got out of the truck and closed the door.

He didn't say anything, just looked at her for a long moment, then put the truck in gear and drove away.

She stood in the yard until he was out of sight, then burst into tears.

Chapter Twelve

She cried until she was empty inside, and then she went to bed and cried herself to sleep. When she woke, her cheeks were still damp with tears. Had she been crying while she slept, too? It wouldn't have surprised her.

She looked at the clock. It was almost four. She should get up, take a shower, change her clothes. Instead, she stared up at the ceiling.

Why had she behaved as if Chay had lied to her? A silly question, she thought, because she felt as if he had lied to her. But it wasn't really a lie. He had made a promise and honored it. Why had she overreacted? Why had she made such a big deal out of it when it was really nothing? Maybe she had just been in shock to discover that she had been right all along. Instead of being upset, she should be glad that he kept his promises, that he was an honorable man, a man of his word.

Trust, she thought, it all boiled down to trust. Rick had betrayed her and now she was afraid to trust Chay. But who could blame her? Chay was tall, dark and handsome. She was, at best, ordinary. He could probably have his pick of women, so why did he want her? She wasn't beautiful. She didn't have any special talents. She wasn't even a very good cook.

And there was the real problem, she thought. She lacked self-esteem. But then, she always had. Deep down, she had always known Rick would leave her for someone else, someone better, someone prettier. And that was exactly what he had done. Was that why she had pushed Chay away? Why she had made such a fuss over nothing? So she could leave him before he left her?

"Pathetic," she muttered. "You're pathetic."

Tossing the covers aside, she got out of bed. She was heading for the shower when the phone rang.

Her heart skipped a beat as she ran to answer it. "Hello?"

"Hi, Dana. Is everything all right?"

"Oh. Hi, Mom."

"Are you all right, dear?"

"Oh, sure, I'm fine. How's everything at home? You and Dad okay?"

"What's wrong, Dana?"

She sat down heavily. There was no use trying to fool her mother. Marge Westlake had always known when her daughter was in trouble or in pain. "Oh, Mom, I've made such a mess of things."

"Is this about Rick? He was never right for you. I know this sounds cruel, but I think what happened was for the best. He would never have made you happy."

"It's not about Rick. It's, well, I met a man up here . . ."

There was a barely noticeable pause on the other end of the phone. "Go on."

In a rush, Dana told her mother everything that had happened. All her doubts and fears poured out in a flood of words and tears. "And now," she said, "I don't know what to do."

"I remember Chay," her mother said. "You say he's Big John's son? I met Chay and his mother one summer. He was a good-looking young man, very quiet, as I recall. Very polite. Chay was only, oh, I don't know, fifteen or sixteen I guess. His mother was lovely." Marge paused a moment before asking, "Are you in love with him, Dana?"

"I think so."

"I see."

"You don't approve?"

"I didn't say that. But you've only known the man for a short time. Less than a month. I don't want to see you get hurt again, and I think maybe you're rushing into something you're not quite ready for."

The words flitted through Dana's mind. It wasn't the first time she had wondered if she was making a mistake. But being with Chay didn't feel like a mistake. He made her feel beautiful, desirable. Likable. Rick had said he loved her, but he had always made her feel inadequate, as if she wasn't quite good enough or smart enough or pretty enough. He had made her feel as if anything she thought or wanted wasn't as important as what he thought or wanted. Chay had never made her feel like that. Rick had declared she was beautiful, but she had frequently caught him looking at other women. When she was with Chay, she always had his full attention. When she was with him, she felt as if she was the only woman in the world. And that day at the lake, he had made her feel beautiful.

Why had she acted so foolishly? She

knew why, though she was loath to admit it. She had started a fight and left him before he could leave her. Well, not exactly a fight, she amended, but she had withdrawn from him mentally and physically, and he had known it.

"Dana?"

"What? Oh, sorry, Mom. Listen, I've got to go. Thanks for calling. Give my love to Dad, will you?"

"All right, dear. We'll see you when you get home."

"All right. Bye, Mom."

Dana hung up the phone, then ran to her room and changed her clothes. She had to go see Chay. She had to apologize for her foolish behavior and hope that he would forgive her for acting like a total idiot. She was only going to be up here for a short time, and she wanted to spend as much of the time she had left with Chay.

She only hoped she hadn't shattered the tenuous bond between them.

Chapter Thirteen

Chay stood just inside the door of Big John's bedroom, one shoulder braced against the wall. Sometime in the last few hours the old man had taken a turn for the worse. Chay had summoned the doctor, who had examined Big John, then shook his head. Chay couldn't believe there was no hope left. He had assured Ashley that her father was going to be fine, had believed it himself. Big John had always seemed indestructible. But years of over-indulgence had taken their toll on the old man's heart and now it was just a matter of time.

Ashley sat at her father's bedside, her hand tightly grasping his, her gaze never leaving his face.

"I'm sorry, Daddy. I didn't mean to upset you. Please forgive me. Please don't leave me. I love you."

She had repeated the same words over and over again during the last two hours, convinced that she had somehow caused her father's relapse. Her eyes were red and swollen, her cheeks damp with tears that seemed to have no end. Chay had tried to comfort her, tried to get her to go lie down for a little while, to try to get some sleep, but she refused to leave Big John's side. Looking at the old man, Chay couldn't blame her.

Big John lay unmoving, his eyes closed, his breathing shallow. There was an unhealthy pallor to the man's skin. His cheeks looked sunken. Chay shook his head. Though there had never been any love lost between the two of them, he knew he would miss Big John when he was gone.

The doctor hovered on the far side of the bed, coming forward every fifteen minutes or so to take Big John's blood pressure and listen to his heart. Chay could tell, from the doctor's expression, that there was little hope his patient would recover.

Chay had left the room only once since Big John had lost consciousness, and that had been to put in a call to his mother. She had listened quietly to what he'd had to say, then asked him to send Big John's plane to pick her up.

Chay checked the clock on Big John's nightstand. It was just after five. His mother should be at the ranch within the hour.

Anna Mae tiptoed into the room, bringing a pot of fresh coffee for Chay and the doctor and a cup of hot chocolate for Ashley. She knelt beside Ashley and gave the girl a hug.

"Young Mr. DeHaven called," Anna Mae said. "He's on his way over."

Ashley nodded, but didn't reply.

Rising, Anna Mae looked at Chay, her eyes filled with sorrow. "Is there anything I can do?"

"Just let me know when my mother gets here."

With a nod, Anna Mae left the room.

Chay blew out a sigh. If Big John died, he knew he was going to spend the rest of his life wishing he had tried harder to win his father's acceptance. Muttering an oath, he walked over to the window and stared into the distance. He was twenty-nine years old, and still trying to win his old man's love and approval.

His gaze wandered over the ranch, wondering what would happen to it when Big John died. He had no doubt that Big John had left it all to Ashley, but she was too young to look after the place. One thing was for certain, he couldn't leave here now, not when Ashley would need him more than ever. She would be able to live here year-round now, if she wanted, or she could go and live with her mother. Chay grunted softly. Either way, Chay would have to stay on at the ranch and look out for her best interests until she was old enough, and wise enough, to do it on her own.

He glanced over his shoulder at Ashley. He knew her better than she knew herself, knew she wouldn't leave the ranch now. He wondered if Jillian would move back to the ranch to look after her daughter, wondered if Big John had bequeathed anything to the two women who had borne his children. And Georgia Cookson. No doubt the old man had made provisions for his latest paramour, as well.

Chay blew out a sigh. Deep down in a dark corner of his soul where he didn't look too often, jealousy reared its ugly head. Though he didn't really begrudge the ranch to Ashley, he couldn't help feeling it should rightfully be his — or at least partly his. Whether Big John liked it or not, Chay was his firstborn. No one loved the place the way Chay did. No one else had put in the long hours he had to make sure things ran smoothly. Sure,

Ashley loved the place because it was home, but the ranch was in Chay's blood, as much a part of him as the color of his hair or the dusky hue of his skin. Working on the ranch was more than just a job to Chay. His heart and soul had been poured into every inch of ground.

Chay muttered an oath under his breath, hating the feelings coming to the fore. He had told Dana he stayed because of that thousand acres, but the truth was he would have stayed because he loved the land itself. Dana . . . the rift between them had left an ache in his heart. He knew she was angry with him for no good reason. She acted as if he had lied to her when all he had done was keep a promise he had made. Was that any reason for her to act as if he had betrayed her trust? He thought about it and decided she was just running scared, afraid to get involved with another man so soon after she had been hurt. He could understand that, and maybe he didn't blame her, but he wasn't going to let her go without a fight. She was over-reacting, and when she'd had time to think about it, he was sure she would realize it, too. He wasn't so sure he could convince her that her place was here, with him. She was a city girl, after all, and as much as she seemed to be enjoying her vacation, he didn't know if she would want to live in this part of the country all year long. So, he thought with a wry grin, he would just have to persuade her.

A heart-wrenching sob from Ashley drew Chay's attention. A cold certainty welled in his heart as he turned slowly from the window. Ashley sat at her father's side, shaking her head, murmuring, "No, no, no," while the doctor bent over Big John.

Chay closed the distance between them in two long strides, drew Ashley into his arms and led her out of the room.

"No!" She looked up at him through red-rimmed eyes. "He can't be dead, Chay! Not now. I have to tell him I'm sorry. I have to tell him that I loved him!" She twisted out of his arms, intent on returning to her father's room.

Chay caught her by the hand and drew her into his arms once more. "Ashley, honey, you need to get some sleep."

"I can't! I have to tell him . . . don't you understand? The last thing I told him was that I hated him . . . and . . ."

"He knows you didn't mean it, honey. There's a lot that will need doing in the next few days. You need some rest."

She stared up at him, mute. "It isn't fair. So much has changed so quickly."

"I know." He hugged her close, his heart aching for her loss, for the pain etched in her face. "I'll be here for you, you know that. Your mother is on her way, and so is mine. Everything will be all right." Putting his arm around her shoulders, he led her down the hallway to her bedroom. She sat down on the edge of the bed and he pulled off her shoes and socks, then tucked her into bed. "Go to sleep, honey."

She clung to his hand. "Stay with me."

"All right."

Chay pulled her old rocker up next to the bed and sat down, her hand clasped in his. "He knows you loved him," he said quietly. "He knows you didn't mean any of the things you said, just like you know he loved you, no matter what."

She nodded. "Did you love him, Chay?"

"No, but I respected him."

"He didn't love you, either, did he?"

"No."

"Why not?"

"Maybe because we were so much alike in some ways and so different in others."

"I love you," she said with a yawn. "I've always loved you."

"I know." He brushed a lock of hair from

her forehead. "Go to sleep now."

With a sniff, she closed her eyes. Moments later, she was asleep.

Chay stayed by her side for a long while, watching her sleep. How different their lives had been. Ashley had been treated like a princess her whole life, pampered and spoiled by everyone who knew her, including him, while he'd been forced to pretend he was nothing more to Big John than just another hired hand. Well, as far as he was concerned, people could go on thinking that.

Rising, he brushed a kiss across her forehead. She was likely one of the richest girls in the state now. In a few years, she would be swamped by men, young and old alike, who would be eager to marry her for the ranch alone. Well, he thought as he left her room and closed the door behind him, they would have to come through him first!

Anna Mae was waiting for him at the bottom of the stairs. "We have company," she said, nodding toward the front parlor. "Your mother is here."

Chapter Fourteen

Chay felt himself smiling at the thought of seeing his mother again. He hadn't seen her in over a year and he had missed her.

After thanking Anna Mae, he hurried into the parlor.

At fifty-three, his mother was as beautiful and vibrant as she had been at twenty-three. Her thick black hair fell to her waist. Her skin, a shade darker than his own, was smooth and unlined.

A smile lit her face when he entered the room. *"Naeha,"* she murmured. My son. She opened her arms and he went to her.

"Na-hkoe," he said, embracing her. "How was your flight?"

"A little bumpy," she said with a grimace. "You know how I hate planes."

Chay led her to the sofa and sat down beside her.

"I'm too late, aren't I?" she asked softly.

209

Chay nodded. "He died about an hour ago."

With a sigh, she reached for his hand. "I'll miss him," she said, and he heard the surprise in her voice. "I loved him and I hated him." Tears welled in her eyes. "But I never thought I'd miss him." She wiped away her tears. "Did you two ever make peace?"

"No. He would never let me in." Chay shook his head. "Why did he hate me so much?"

"Because you were everything he wanted to be. He had money, but you had integrity. He had power, but you had courage. He could command people to do his bidding, he could earn their respect, but never their devotion. And I suspect part of his hatred for you was because of me, because I turned my back on everything he could give me and walked away. He never forgave me for that." Her fingertips slid down his cheek. "You were a constant reminder to him of what I'd done. How's Ashley taking it?"

"Not very well. They had a fight just before his attack. She's feeling guilty, blaming herself for what happened."

"Have you called her mother?"

"Yes, she's on her way."

"Is there anything I can do?"

"I don't know. I haven't thought that far ahead."

"Why don't you let me take care of the funeral arrangements."

"Are you sure?"

"Of course. I'll talk to Anna Mae and get a list of people who need to be told."

"Thanks, *Na-hkoe*."

"I'd like to go freshen up a little if it's all right."

"Sure." Rising, he offered her his hand. "I had Anna Mae make up your old room for you," he said, then frowned. "Maybe you'd rather not stay there."

"No, it will be fine." She smiled up at him. "Not all my memories are bad. Is dinner still at eight?"

Chay nodded.

"I'll see you then."

"Right. Let Anna Mae know if you need anything."

He walked her to the staircase, then, in need of some space and fresh air, he left the house.

Feeling restless, he went down to the barn and saddled his favorite horse. He had a good three hours until dinner. There was nothing to be done this afternoon. The doctor had made arrangements to have Big

John's body taken into town. His mother would take care of all of the funeral arrangements. The foreman would make sure the ranch work got done.

Swinging into the saddle, Chay rode out of the yard. He told himself he was just going for a short ride even as he turned his mount toward the path that led to Dana's place. He just hoped she was still there.

Dana got out of the car and stared at the rear right tire. Of all times to get a flat, why did it have to be now? Muttering under her breath, she kicked the tire, wincing as pain lanced through her big toe.

Grimacing, she limped over to the porch and sat on the bottom step. She could call Chay, but she really needed to see him, to apologize face-to-face, although doing it over the phone would undoubtedly be easier, especially if he wouldn't forgive her.

She stared into the distance, wondering if she was making a mistake. Maybe her mother was right and she was just setting herself up to be hurt again. Maybe she should just pack up and go back to Ashton Falls where she belonged. She couldn't hide up here forever. Sooner or later she had to go home and face her friends and family, endure their sympathy and their snickers and get on with living.

She looked over her shoulder, thinking that she would miss this house, this place, but most of all, she would miss Chay, the crinkle around his eyes, the touch of his hand in her hair, the way he sometimes whispered her name, the sound of his laughter, his kisses that were more potent than the oncoming storm.

She glanced up as lightning flashed across the skies followed by a low rumble of thunder. Dark clouds scudded across the sky. Another bolt of lightning sizzled through the heavens, unleashing a sudden downpour.

Jumping to her feet, Dana ran up the porch steps, then stood in the doorway, watching the rain come down.

She was about to go into the house when she saw something move just beyond the trees.

Peering through the downpour, she saw a horse and rider emerge from the woods, felt her heart skip a beat as she recognized the rider.

It was Chay.

He dismounted in a single lithe motion and ground-tied his mount, then ascended the steps two at a time. He stood on the porch, hat in hand. Raindrops rolled off the brim and splattered on the porch at his feet.

Dana gazed at him, speechless, her hands itching to reach for him, yet something held her immobile.

"I would have told you if I could," he said. "I'm sorry."

"It was silly of me to expect you to go back on your word. I'm sorry."

They spoke simultaneously, the tension between them evaporating as soon as the words were said.

"Come on in," Dana said. "Let me get you something hot to drink." Taking his hat, she hung it on the hook inside the door. Feeling as if a load had been removed from her shoulders, she led the way into the kitchen.

Chay followed her, then stopped in the doorway. "Dana."

She turned at the sound of her name, knew what he was going to say even before he spoke.

"He's gone," Chay said, his voice heavy with regret.

"Oh, Chay, I'm so sorry." Taking him by the hand, she went into the living room. Sitting on the sofa, she drew him down beside her and put her arms around him.

He rested his forehead against hers. "It's

so hard to believe he's gone. He seemed so strong. Indomitable." He swallowed hard, his hand reaching for hers. "I waited all my life to hear him call me his son, to tell me that he loved me. It'll never happen now."

She didn't know what to say. Except for her grandparents, she had never lost anyone close to her. A sob racked his body. She held him close as his pain washed over her. For all that Chay had said he didn't love Big John, the tears in his eyes proved otherwise.

He was quiet for several minutes and then he drew away. "I'm sorry," he said somewhat sheepishly. "I haven't cried since I was six."

"You don't have to apologize or be embarrassed. No matter how you felt about him or how he felt about you, he was still your father."

"Yeah." He blew out a soul-deep sigh. "I'm going to be pretty busy for the next couple of days, and then we need to talk."

"All right."

His gaze searched her face. "You'll still be here? You're not leaving?"

"No," she said. "I'm not leaving." And she knew, in that moment, that if he asked her, she would stay here, with him, for as long as he wanted her.

"I've got to get back," he said. "My mother's at the ranch. I'd like for you to meet her."

His words warmed her heart. "I'd like that."

He kissed her lightly, then gained his feet. Moving toward the front door, he picked up his hat, ran his fingers around the brim.

"What is it?" she asked.

"I'd . . . would you come to the funeral? I'd like for you to be there."

"Of course."

"I'll call you and let you know when it is."

She nodded, then rose on tiptoe and kissed him. "I think I love the rain," she said. "It always seems to bring us together."

He smiled faintly, then left the house.

As always, she stood on the porch and watched him until he was out of sight.

Chapter Fifteen

The funeral was held at eleven o'clock on Wednesday morning. Dana hadn't seen Chay since he came to her house the Sunday before. She regretted each day without him.

The memorial service for Big John was, as expected, the biggest one the town had ever seen. The pretty, old-fashioned church on Sycamore Street was filled to capacity. In addition to family and friends, it looked as if practically every man, woman and child in Wardman's Hollow had turned out to pay their respects to the town's leading citizen. Newspaper reporters hovered outside like vultures, hoping to get a word with a member of the family.

The immediate family sat in the front pew. Dana sat on Chay's right. Ashley sat on his left. Ashley's mother sat beside her daughter, and Chay's mother sat beside Dana.

Dana couldn't help thinking that Big John's taste in women varied greatly. Ashley's mother, Jillian, looked like a fashion model. She was tall, willowy and blond, with clear blue eyes and a flawless complexion. Chay's mother, Claudia, whom Dana had met only briefly, was not quite so tall or willowy but she was equally beautiful, with large dark eyes and smooth dusky skin. Dana felt overshadowed by both women.

Big John's mistress sat across the aisle and several rows back. She wore a demure black dress and a large black hat with a veil. Dana couldn't help wondering how many of the other black-clad women scattered throughout the church had had affairs with Chay's father.

Glancing around, Dana spotted LuAnn, Megan and Brittany a few rows back. Brandon DeHaven was also there.

During the service, several people got up to speak, relating the details of Big John's life, telling how he had inherited the Bar W from his widowed mother at a young age, how the ranch had prospered under his hand. They spoke of his shrewd business sense, his larger-than-life sense of humor that was matched only by his temper, his generosity.

Dana tried to pay attention to what was being said, but she was distracted by Chay's nearness, by the way he held himself, stiff and unmoving, as if he was afraid that any show of emotion would be his undoing. Ashley leaned against him, weeping softly into a handkerchief. Jillian wept along with her daughter. Claudia listened intently to what was said, her face impassive, her hands clasped tightly in her lap.

There was a short service at the graveside, and then the family and those who had been invited drove out to the ranch for lunch.

While standing near the long buffet tables that practically groaned beneath the weight of food and drink, Dana couldn't help overhearing bits and pieces of stories and anecdotes about Big John. He had, indeed, been bigger than life. Whether people loved him or hated him, they had all respected him.

She was feeling rather out of place as the afternoon wore on. Sitting in the living room, surrounded by friends of the family, none of whom she knew, she wondered why she had let Chay talk her into coming. Except for Chay and Ashley and Ashley's friends, she didn't know a soul. The couple nearest her were speculating about just how much money Ashley stood to inherit, and who would run the ranch now that Big John was gone. Both agreed that Ashley was far too young to run the place. The woman wondered if Jillian would move back to the ranch and stay with Ashley. The man wondered if Big John had left anything to his assorted mistresses.

With a sigh, Dana glanced into the other room. She could see Chay there, talking with several people. He nodded at something one of them said, accepted a hug from another. She wished she had brought her own car so she could go home.

Rising, she made her way through the kitchen and out to the backyard. No matter what happened after today, it was sure to make a big change in Chay's life. Knowing him as she did, she knew that he would feel obligated to look after his sister and the ranch. No doubt he would be extremely busy for the next few months. Then, too, he had his own place to look after.

She was standing by one of the corrals, petting a pretty, little brown-and-white pony, when she heard footsteps behind her. She turned, hoping it was Chay seeking her out. Instead, she saw his mother walking toward her.

"I saw you leave and thought this might be a good time for us to get acquainted," Claudia said, coming up beside Dana.

Dana nodded.

"Chay seems rather smitten with you, though I understand you've only known each other for a couple of weeks."

"I'm rather smitten with him, as well," Dana confessed.

"He's a good man, my son."

"Yes, he is."

"He's had a difficult life," Claudia said, then shook her head. "I'm not saying this well. I don't mean that he's been neglected or abused, only that he was never able to have the one thing he wanted the most."

"His father's love," Dana said.

"He told you that?"

"Yes. I asked him once, before I knew that Big John was his father, why he stayed on at the ranch. He said it was a good job. I know now that it was so much more."

Claudia nodded. "He loves the land. He loves Ashley. And even though he'll never admit it, even to himself, he loved his father. When Chay was a little boy, I tried to make it up to him but there comes a time when a boy needs his father, when he needs a man's example to guide him. But

Big John didn't have time for a son who was not only half-Indian, but who had been born on the wrong side of the blanket. Oh, he provided for us. Big John's pride wouldn't let his son do without, but Chay didn't want clothes or a pony, he wanted his father's attention, and that was something he never had. To tell you the truth, sometimes I'm surprised that Chay turned out so well."

"Did you want to marry Big John?" Dana asked.

"No." She smiled. "And a good thing it was, too, because he never would have married me. He was angry when I left, but I couldn't stay any longer. Chay was grown by then and he didn't need me anymore."

Dana smiled, remembering how Chay had said he hadn't gone to Arizona with his mother because she hadn't needed him anymore.

"So, how serious is it between you and my son?"

"It isn't. Not at all. I mean, I hardly know him." She knew she was babbling, felt her cheeks grow hot under Claudia's pointed stare. "Perhaps if we had more time . . . I . . . It's just . . ."

"You're in love with him, aren't you?"

Dana nodded. "But it doesn't matter. I'm leaving on Friday."

"So soon?"

"I have to be at work next Monday." She smiled wistfully. "Anyway, I don't belong here. I don't think I was cut out to be a country wife."

"I see." Claudia glanced over Dana's shoulder. "Here comes Chay now. It was a pleasure meeting you, Dana. I hope everything works out for you."

"Thank you."

Claudia squeezed Dana's hand then turned and walked toward the house.

Butterflies danced in Dana's stomach as she watched Chay stop to speak briefly with his mother, then continue toward her. She loved watching him, loved the way he moved, like some large jungle cat on the prowl, always so self-assured, so confident.

"Here you are," he said. "I've been looking everywhere for you."

She shrugged. "I, well, I felt out of place, you know?"

"I'm sorry. I shouldn't have left you alone."

"No, it's all right, really. You needed to be there. How's Ashley doing?"

"She's still pretty shaken up, but she'll

be okay. She's Big John's daughter, after all."

"Yes."

His gaze moved over her. "When are you leaving?"

"Friday morning."

"Any chance you could stay a little longer?"

"No, I'm afraid not."

He muttered an oath, his expression turbulent. "I had a feeling you'd say that. Knowing how stubborn you can be, I was going to follow you home."

"You were?"

"Yeah."

"But you've changed your mind?" Disappointment sat like a lead weight on her heart. She would have loved to spend more time with him, to show him around Ashton Falls, to introduce him to her friends.

He folded his arms over the top rail of the corral. "The lawyer came to the house last night and read the will."

"Oh? I suppose Big John left everything to Ashley."

"Not exactly. He left half of the place to me on the provision that I stay here and look after her until she marries or until she turns twenty-one."

"That's wonderful!" Dana exclaimed.

"I'm happy for you, Chay, really I am." It was something he would have done anyway, she thought.

He nodded. The terms of the old man's will had been so unexpected, he wasn't sure how he felt. He had been tempted to give his share to Ashley and walk away. Even if he'd had to leave the ranch, he would have been close enough to look after her anyway. Damn the old man! Was this Big John's way of trying to make up for a lifetime of neglect? Well, it was too damn late! The old man didn't have to leave him a damn thing. Chay had always looked after Ashley. Big John didn't have to bribe him to stay and do what he'd done most of his life. He had told Ashley as much later that night, but, bless her heart, she had said it was only right, after all, and that he deserved more than half the ranch, that it should all have been his in the first place. After all was said and done, Chay knew he couldn't turn his back on the land or on his sister. He loved them both and, except for his mother, Ashley was the only family he had.

"Anyway," he said, "I can't leave the ranch now. I've got a lot of paperwork to take care of, and I need to go over the ranch accounts."

Dana nodded.

"Jillian's going to stay for a week or two, but then she'll be heading back to Salt Lake. Anyway, you can see why I can't take off."

"Of course," Dana said. She forced a smile, hoping he couldn't see how her heart was breaking. "Ashley will need you more than ever after her mother goes home."

But, oh, she thought, *I need you, too.*

Turning away from the fence, Chay drew her into his arms. "I'll miss you."

"I'll miss you, too."

"Will you write me when you get home?" he asked.

"Sure."

"Maybe we could go out to dinner to-morrow night . . . no, I forgot, I'm supposed to be taking Ashley and Jillian and my mother out to dinner. Why don't you come with us?"

"No, I don't think so. Anyway, I need to pack and close up the house."

He nodded. "Come on. I'll take you home."

She sat close to him in the truck on the way home, thinking how much she would miss him. He had said he would miss her, too, and perhaps he would, though she wondered when he'd have the time. Be-tween settling the estate, running the ranch and looking after Ashley, he wasn't going to have a lot of spare time on his hands.

Chay walked her to her door, then drew her into his arms. She nestled against him and he thought how right it felt for her to be there. His nostrils filled with her scent — cologne and shampoo and woman. He had never felt this way about any of the women he had dated, but then, he had been careful in his choice of dates, making sure the relationship stayed casual, never letting things get serious. But Dana was different. He had known that from the first.

"Listen," he said, "once things quiet down around here and Ashley's feeling better, I should be able to take some time off. What would you say if I came to Ashton Falls for a couple of days?"

"I'd like that."

"This isn't goodbye, Dana. I won't let it be goodbye. I'll be there as soon as I can get away."

She nodded. "Don't forget about me."

"No, I won't."

He kissed her then, a slow deep kiss that he hoped conveyed what he felt deep inside but seemed unable to put into words.

There were tears in her eyes when he broke the kiss.

He hoped that was a good sign.

Chapter Sixteen

Dana stood in the middle of her apartment. It seemed smaller somehow. Though she had only been gone for three weeks, it seemed like years since she had been home. The place hadn't changed, she realized, but she had.

Chay might never call. She might never see him again. But he had given her a sense of self-worth, made her feel beautiful, worthwhile.

Blinking back tears, she unpacked, took a long hot shower, then pulled on her nightgown and sat down to write him a letter. She had known, as soon as she walked in the front door, that she had made a mistake. Jobs came and went, but a man like Chayton Lone Elk was one of a kind. He had never said he loved her. She had never said she loved him. But there was definitely something between them, something wonderful and rare and worth pursuing.

Going to the front window, she looked out into the night. Neon lights shone on the blacktop. Houses, like boxes, lined the far side of the street. A few palm trees grew along the sidewalk. A few stars twinkled in the sky. There were no deer grazing along the edge of her property. She couldn't see the Milky Way. There were no pine trees. There would be no birds singing in the morning, no squirrels darting from tree to tree, no eagles soaring in the sky. Chay wouldn't come knocking at her door.

Sitting at the kitchen table, she found a sheet of paper and a pen and began to write, telling him how much she had enjoyed their time together, how much she was looking forward to seeing him again if he found the time to come to Ashton Falls.

Sitting back, she relived all the good times they had had, the way he made her feel, his concern for Ashley, the pain he had tried to hide when his father died.

"I love him," she murmured. "I love everything about him."

And it was time to tell him so. But not on paper. She tore up the letter and tossed it in the trash. She went to the phone and picked up the receiver, but a phone call didn't seem right, either.

Smiling, her heart soaring, she danced around the apartment, laughing out loud. Tomorrow, she was going to quit her job and move to Wardman's Hollow. It might be the biggest mistake she ever made . . . no, Rick was the biggest mistake she had ever made, she thought, grinning. But, right or wrong, she was going to follow her heart back to Wardman's Hollow.

Before she met Chay, she would never have had the nerve to do such a thing, to open herself up to rejection, but Chay was worth it. And if it turned out he didn't love her, well, he had given her the courage to overcome that, too.

Her boss couldn't believe it when she told him she was handing in her two weeks' notice. He ranted and raved and then begged her to stay. In the end, he wished her well, wrote her a reference so flattering it sounded as if she had written it herself, and gave her an extra two weeks' severance pay "because she deserved it." Her mother and father couldn't believe it when she told them she was moving to Wardman's Hollow, permanently. They both tried to talk her out of it. Her father told her she was being too impetuous — something she had never been before. Her mother told her to wait a few weeks, to let Chay make the first move, to think of what she was doing, what she was giving up. But Dana couldn't wait. Deep in her heart, she knew it was the right thing to do.

She spent the next two weeks sorting through her belongings, putting them into two piles — things she was taking, things she was leaving behind. She called the utility companies and told them she was moving, canceled the newspaper, and did the hundred and one other things that had to be taken care of.

Her last morning at home, she packed up everything she was taking with her, hauled the rest of it to the Goodwill, told her parents she would see them at Christmas, then jumped in her car and headed back to Wardman's Hollow.

It was late Sunday night when she reached the house nestled in the hills. For a moment, she sat in the car, looking up at the house. Home, she thought, this was home now.

Bags in hand, she paused on the top step of the front porch to look at the sky. The night was breathtakingly clear. The Milky Way stretched overhead like a pathway through the heavens. Millions of stars winked at her. A bright yellow moon hung low in the sky.

Going inside, her first thought was to call Chay and tell him she was back, but then she decided to wait. This wasn't something that should be said in a telephone call. She wanted to see his face when she told him she loved him, wanted to see his eyes.

Unable to sit still, she went through the house, removing the dustcovers from the furniture. Going into the bedroom, she put her clothes away, then stowed her suitcases in the back of the closet. Whatever happened, she wouldn't be needing them again right away.

Later, she wandered through the house, deciding where to put her unicorn collection, the painting she had bought from an art gallery last year. It was her favorite piece, and now she knew why. It depicted a warrior astride a big black horse, a warrior who looked remarkably like Chay. She hung the picture over the fireplace, found herself looking at it over and over again as she moved through the house.

It was only later, lying in bed, that doubts assailed her.

What if she was wrong?

What if he didn't love her the way she loved him?

★ ★ ★

Monday morning Chay sat in the kitchen, a mug of coffee cupped in his hands as he watched Anna Mae teach Ashley how to make a pumpkin pie. Ashley should have been at school, but she'd caught the sniffles over the weekend and he'd decided to let her stay home one more day. It touched a chord deep within him to hear his sister laugh at something Anna Mae said. He had let Ashley stay home from school the week following the funeral and then, hoping to cheer her up, he had invited the Three Musketeers over for the weekend. It had done Ashley a world of good to spend time with her friends and her mother.

Ashley had asked her mother to stay on at the ranch, but Jillian had refused. Her life was in Salt Lake with her husband, she'd said, but Ashley was more than welcome to come and stay with her. Chay had been a little surprised when Ashley decided to stay on at the ranch. But then, maybe it wasn't such a surprise. Ashley had never cared for Jillian's husband.

Chay blew out a sigh. It wasn't easy, running the ranch, taking care of the books, making sure the cowhands were doing their jobs, keeping an eye on his sister . . .

He grinned inwardly. His sister. Word of his relationship to Ashley and Big John had spread through Wardman's Hollow like wildfire. Jillian and his mother had ordered Big John's headstone and now it was carved in white marble for all the world to see:

John Matthew Wardman,
beloved father of
Ashley Marie and Chayton Lone Elk.

The people in town and at the ranch looked at him differently now. He wasn't just one of Big John's hired hands. He was half owner of one of the biggest cattle ranches in this part of the country. Yes, people looked at him differently, and he wasn't sure he liked it. He was still the same, yet even as the thought crossed his mind, he knew he wasn't. He had responsibilities now. Sometimes he felt as if he was carrying the weight of the world on his shoulders, felt as if everyone was watching him, waiting for him to fail. He had been a cowhand all his life. Now, suddenly, he was responsible for the success or failure of a ranch that had prospered for generations.

He stared into the mug cradled in his hands as if he could see the ranch's future in the coffee cooling inside.

Muttering an oath, he set the cup on the table. He wasn't really worried about the ranch. He wasn't worried about Ashley. And he didn't give a hoot in hell about what the cowhands or the people in town thought of him. The only thing he was worried about was Dana and whether they had a future together. Well, he had waited long enough to find out. Next week he was driving down to Ashton Falls to see Dana. He was going to tell her how he felt, ask her to give them a chance. If he had to, he'd go down on his knees and beg, though he hoped it wouldn't come to that.

He shook his head. He hadn't been this infatuated with a woman since he fell head over heels for his sixth-grade teacher and even that didn't compare to this. He had never known a woman like Dana, couldn't forget the awareness that sizzled between them whenever they touched. Though he had only known her a few short weeks, she had carved a place for herself in his life and in his heart that he knew no other woman would ever be able to fill. He couldn't stop thinking about her, couldn't stop wanting her. It was more than mere desire, more than just physical hunger. He knew what that felt like, and what he felt for Dana was as far from lust as the sun from the moon.

He swore under his breath. He couldn't explain his attraction for her any more than he could ignore it. He only knew he felt incomplete without her.

Pushing away from the table, he grabbed his hat off the rack and left the house.

Ten minutes later, he was riding toward her house in the hills, drawn by a sudden need to walk the land where she had walked.

Dana glanced at the clock, willing the hands to move. She had been up for hours, unable to sleep, unable to think of anything but seeing Chay again. She glanced at the clock for what must have been the tenth time in as many minutes. Eleven-fifteen. She had been about to leave the house when she realized that Chay would be at work by now, probably out on the range somewhere, branding cattle or whatever cowboys did during the day. Why hadn't she thought of that sooner? She frowned. Maybe he didn't do cowboy work now that he owned half the ranch.

Whatever he was doing, she wouldn't be able to see him until tonight.

She stamped her foot in frustration.

How was she supposed to wait until then? What if she lost her nerve?

Feeling as though the walls were closing in on her, she pulled on a heavy jacket and a pair of gloves and went out onto the front porch. She paced back and forth for several minutes, then dropped into the porch rocker. She couldn't just sit here all day. Maybe she would drive into town and pick up some groceries or take in a movie. Or buy a new dress. Yes, a new dress to wear for Chay, something that would knock his boots off!

She was about to go into the house when Chay emerged from the trees.

She stopped, frozen in place at the sight of him. He sat tall and straight in the saddle, his black hat pulled low over his eyes, his broad shoulders filling out the heavy sheepskin jacket he wore. Her heart quickened as she drank in the sight of him. He was here, she thought, and then wondered what he was doing there. Had someone told him she had returned? But that was impossible. No one knew she was here except her parents and they certainly wouldn't have called to tell him.

Excitement fluttered in her stomach as he reined his horse to a halt in front of the porch. He pushed his hat back on his head, then sat there, looking up at her. It was hard to think, hard to breathe, with his dark gaze fixed on her face, and then he dismounted in a single fluid movement.

He was here. Every fiber of her being, every cell in her body, yearned for him. She hardly knew the man, and yet, in some ways, she felt as if she had known him all her life. She had been attracted to him from the first, drawn to him in ways she had never been drawn to any other man she had ever met.

He ground-reined his horse, swung out of the saddle, vaulted the porch rail, lifted her from the rocker and kissed her.

Her eyelids fluttered down, her senses reeling with his nearness, the heat of his kiss, the shelter of his arms around her. How had she ever thought she could live without him? He was as necessary as the very air that she breathed.

She whimpered in protest when he took his mouth from hers.

"Be quiet," he admonished, and then he was kissing her again, stealing the strength from her legs so that she leaned against him, her arms tight around his waist, her body seeking to be closer to his, though she was certain that was impossible.

She gazed up at him when he broke the kiss.

His gaze trapped hers, his eyes dark and intense upon her face. He was holding her so tight, she could almost feel the beat of his heart. "We belong together, Dana. I know it. I can feel it."

She started to say she agreed, but Chay put his hand over her mouth, stilling her words. Was he perhaps afraid that she might disagree?

"Search your heart," he went on. "You know it's true."

Joy filled her heart, soared through her soul. She removed his hand from her mouth. "Of course I know it's true," she said, laughing. "Why do you think I came back?"

"I don't know. Why did you come back?"

"To tell you that I love you."

He blinked at her. "You do?"

She nodded.

"You're sure? We hardly know each other."

She frowned at him. "Wait a minute. Didn't you just say we belonged together?"

"Yeah, but I thought you'd argue with me. I was prepared to drag you back to the Bar W and lock you in my bedroom until you agreed that I was right." He laughed sheepishly. "Guess I wasn't prepared for you to give in so quickly."

"I wasn't, either, but the minute I got back to Ashton Falls, I knew leaving here had been a mistake. I started to write you a letter, but I threw it away. Then I thought I'd call, but . . ." She shrugged. "I wanted to see your face when I told you. And if it turned out that you felt the same way, I wanted to see your face when you told me you loved me. Do you love me, Chay?"

"With all my heart."

"Say it."

"I love you, Dana. I'll love you as long as I live. I can't promise that I'll never hurt you or that I won't let you down once in a while, but I'll never betray you and I'll never leave you. I swear it on all I hold dear."

"I believe you."

"Then you'll marry me?"

"Yes, any day you say, anywhere you say."

He let out a war whoop that would have sent shivers down a settler's spine. It sent shivers down her spine, too, shivers of delight. And then he swept her into his arms again, his mouth claiming hers, branding her as his for all time.

Chapter Seventeen

Between planning the wedding and spending as much time as she could with Chay, the next few weeks passed quickly. Dana's parents were less than thrilled to learn that their daughter was going to marry a man she had known such a short time. Even the fact that he owned half of the biggest cattle ranch in Montana couldn't mollify her father. Her mother tried, in a nice way, to convince Dana to wait a year, six months at the least, "just to make sure, dear."

Dana agreed that she had only known Chay a short time but as someone had once said, hearts weren't concerned with clocks or calendars. Besides, she knew couples who had dated for two years or more who ended up divorced. A long courtship didn't ensure a lasting marriage. And she knew in her heart of hearts that she was doing the right thing. For the first time in her life, she had no doubts, no second thoughts, and though she listened politely and patiently to her parents' well-meant advice, she was too much in love to be swayed by their disapproval. They had agreed to be there, and that was all that mattered.

Chay wanted to be married before Christmas so that they could spend it together as man and wife, and Dana had agreed. They set the date for the week before Christmas. Her mother, still hoping to change Dana's mind, had taken the opportunity to suggest that they might want to wait until spring, reminding Dana that Chay had just buried his father and some might consider it unseemly, maybe even disrespectful, for Chay to marry so soon, but Chay had brushed her mother's concerns aside. He didn't want to wait, and neither did Dana, but they both agreed that a small wedding, with just family and a few close friends, would be appropriate, considering the circumstances.

One Saturday afternoon, Dana picked Ashley up at the ranch and they went shopping for Dana's wedding dress. Ashley had been rather subdued on the ride to town, but once Dana started trying on dresses, Ashley got into the spirit of it. She started bringing in the most outrageous dresses for Dana to try on and before long, they were both laughing hysterically.

A short time later, the saleslady brought in a dress with a square neck and a fitted bodice. It had a slim skirt that was longer in the back than in the front. They both knew it was the right one when Dana tried it on.

"Wait until Chay sees it," Ashley said. "You'll knock his socks off."

Dana smiled. "That's what I had in mind."

"You love him, don't you?"

"Well, I hope so. I'm marrying the man."

"Do you think Chay's right about Nick?"

"Yes, I do. Why don't you give Brandon a chance?"

Ashley shrugged. "We've known each other for years. Do you think it's possible to know someone too well?"

"No. Anyway, I'm sure you'll fall in love a thousand times before you meet Mr. Right."

Ashley rolled her eyes. "That's what Chay says, too."

"Well, if two people tell you you're sick, lie down."

"What?"

"Never mind. Help me out of this dress

and I'll buy you lunch."

A short time later they were seated in a small café sipping iced tea. It was a cozy place. Red-and-white checked cloths covered the tables. Matching curtains hung at the windows. There were framed pictures of country singers on the wall, along with old-fashioned signs and posters.

"I still can't believe that no one ever told me Chay was my brother," Ashley remarked.

"It must have been hard for you, finding out the way you did."

"Yeah. I'm glad, though. I've been pretending that he was my brother ever since I was a little girl."

Dana smiled. "He told me how you were always following him around. I always wished I'd had a big brother. It's lonesome, being an only child. I didn't mind so much when I was little. It was kind of fun, getting all the attention and all the presents. My folks always made a big fuss over me, but now I really wish I had some brothers and sisters."

"I'm glad you're marrying Chay. You don't think he'll send me away to school after you get married, do you?"

"Why would he do that?"

"I don't know." Ashley bit down on her

lower lip. "With you here, he might not want me around anymore."

"Don't be silly! He loves you very much."

"You won't mind having me there, will you?"

"Of course not! Didn't I just tell you I wished I had a sister?"

Ashley looked relieved. "Are you nervous about getting married?"

"A little."

"Is Chay . . . never mind."

"Is Chay what?" Dana asked, then gasped. "Ashley!"

"Well, is he?"

"I don't know."

"You've never slept with him?"

Dana shook her head, unable to believe she was having this conversation with a sixteen-year-old girl. A girl who probably knew more about the matter than she did. It was embarrassing.

"What about that other guy? The one you were engaged to before?"

"No, never. And aren't I glad now?"

"Are you still —" Ashley leaned forward and lowered her voice "— a virgin?"

Dana nodded, wondering why she suddenly felt as if she was confessing to something unnatural.

Ashley shook her head. "I don't believe it."

"Does that mean . . . you and Nick haven't . . . have you?" Dana asked, dreading the answer.

"No. He wanted to, but . . . well, I just wasn't ready."

Dana breathed a sigh of relief.

"I guess that's why I like Brandon so much," Ashley said. "He doesn't pressure me. Of course, he wants to do it, too, so he's not that much different than Nick."

"They all want to," Dana said with a grin. "But smart girls, especially teenage girls, wait. It's a precious gift, you know, and shouldn't be given away. Once it's gone, you can't get it back, so you need to be sure, Ashley, really sure."

Dana blew out a sigh, then reached for her drink. She was glad beyond measure that she hadn't given in to Rick. What a huge mistake that would have been!

"I guess you're right," Ashley said. "I never really thought of it that way. It seems like most of the girls in my class have gone all the way at least once. Most of them weren't that impressed, and I know a lot of them were sorry, afterward."

"It doesn't mean anything if there's no love between the man and the woman,"

Dana said. "My mom told me that when I was about your age. It's something I never forgot."

Ashley nodded. "My friend Jenny did it with some guy she knew and she got pregnant. She didn't even love Jeff, she just wanted to see what all the fuss was about. She just had the baby a couple of months ago. A little girl. Her parents wanted her to give the baby away, but she wouldn't. She had to quit school so she could take care of it."

Dana nodded. "It happens all the time. On a happier note," she said, smiling, "I need a maid of honor. Would you like to stand up with me?"

"Me? You want me?"

"Very much."

"Oh, wow! That would be great."

"Wonderful."

"What kind of dress do I get to wear? Something long and pretty?"

"If you want. I was thinking of midnight blue. What do you think?"

"Sounds perfect." Ashley quickly drank the rest of her iced tea. "Can we look today?"

Later that night, wrapped in Chay's arms in front of a toasty fire, Dana told him about her trip to town with Ashley.

He chuckled softly on hearing the note of embarrassment she couldn't keep out of her voice as she related the rather startling conversation that she'd had with Ashley.

"Well," he said, "she won't listen to anything I say. Maybe she'll listen to you."

"I hope so." She stared at the flames, thinking how quickly one's life could change. Not long ago, she had been certain she would never fall in love again.

"Just think, this time next week, you'll be Mrs. Chayton Lone Elk."

Excitement bubbled within her. "It sounds wonderful, doesn't it?"

"I think so."

She looked up at him, admiring the strong lines of his face, the love she saw in his eyes. "I don't think I've ever been this happy," she remarked, "not even the day I won the spelling bee in sixth grade."

"Gee, thanks."

"Hey, that was a big day for me."

Chay grunted. "At least I'm in the top two."

He looked so crestfallen, Dana burst out laughing. "I'm kidding, silly. I've never been this happy in my whole life. Never!"

"That's better," he said, and crushed her close, his mouth seeking hers in what she had come to think of as his caveman kiss. It was long and hard and totally uncivilized, and it always made her toes curl.

Chay released her with a sigh. "I'd better get going. I've got an early day tomorrow."

He kissed the tip of her nose. "Unlike some people I know, I can't sleep until noon."

She punched him on the arm. "I wish! I have a ton of last-minute errands to run."

"Okay, okay." Chay rubbed his arm. "Is this the kind of abuse I have to look forward to?"

Looking properly contrite, Dana kissed his arm. "There. Does that make it better?"

"No, but this will." He kissed her until she couldn't breathe, then rose to his feet, drawing her with him. "Behave yourself, woman."

"Yes, master," she said, and stuck her tongue out at him.

Laughing softly, Chay left the house.

Chapter Eighteen

And suddenly it was her wedding day. Dana woke with a smile on her face. She lay in bed for several minutes, contemplating the day ahead, silently thanking Rick for leaving her. If he hadn't been such a jerk, she might be married to him now instead of engaged to the most wonderful man she had ever known.

She glanced at the clock, gasped when she saw the time. Bill Jenkins, one of the ranch hands, would be there in less than three hours to drive her to the church. Throwing back the covers, she hurried into the bathroom. So much to do, and so little time to do it!

Dana was putting the finishing touches on her makeup when Jenkins arrived.

She took a last look in the mirror, grabbed her suitcase and overnight bag, and hurried out the door.

Chay looked out the window of the limo,

glanced at his watch, drummed his fingers on the armrest. It was his wedding day. Somehow, he hadn't expected to be this nervous about something he had been anticipating for weeks.

Derek, his best man, chuckled softly. "Wedding jitters getting to you?"

"Of course not!" Chay snapped.

Derek laughed. "It's normal. I've never known any man who didn't have a few second thoughts right before the ceremony. Of course, I've known a few men who never made it to the ceremony, too."

Chay grunted. He supposed he was having second thoughts, but not about marrying Dana. He was suddenly afraid that he wouldn't measure up to what she expected, that she might be disappointed or that, in time, she'd be like Ashley's mother and take off, declaring she didn't want to be a ranch wife anymore. Maybe Dana's mother was right. Maybe they should have waited a while, given Dana a little more time to see what it was like, living on the ranch. Dana had said it herself. She was a city girl, and even though the ranch had all the modern conveniences anyone could ask for and they lived near a good-size town, the big city was a good distance away and he didn't get there often in the dead of winter.

Chay swallowed hard. Maybe he was just kidding himself. Maybe he wasn't ready. Or maybe Derek was right, and it was just a case of wedding day jitters. Whatever it was, he didn't like it.

Where was he?

Trying to appear calm, Dana stood in front of the mirror and made a minor adjustment to her veil. Where was he? He should have been there twenty-five minutes ago. The guests were getting restless. The organist had started repeating her repertoire.

Where was he?

Dana looked at her mother and Ashley. Marge's expression was sympathetic. Ashley shrugged and glanced away.

"He'll be here," Dana said. "I know he will. Something must have delayed him."

"He could have called," her mother remarked.

Dana bit down on her lower lip. She wouldn't let doubts eat away at her. She believed in Chay, believed in their love. He could have been detained at the ranch, his best man could have been late, he could have . . .

Changed his mind. The words whispered

through the back of her mind. She shook them off resolutely. Chay wasn't like Rick. Chay loved her.

She clung to that knowledge, refusing to give in to her doubts.

Ten minutes later, there was a knock at the door and the wedding coordinator entered the room. "The groom's here at last," she said, smiling. "And I must say, he's worth waiting for. Are you ready?"

"Yes," Dana replied with a smile. She sent a look that clearly said *I told you so* to her mother, then took up her bouquet and followed the wedding planner toward the chapel.

Chay ran a comb through his hair, blew out a sigh of relief. He had been half-afraid that by the time he made it to the church, Dana would have written him off as a lost cause, packed up and gone back to Ashton Falls once and for all.

He glanced in the mirror, straightened his tie, dusted off his jacket.

"You look fine," Derek said. "You ready?"

"More than ready," Chay said, and opened the door that led into the chapel.

A hush fell over the crowd as Chay and Derek took their places at the altar.

Chay took a deep breath. The organist started playing and Ashley walked down the aisle. She carried a bouquet of pink and white roses. She looked lovely and all grown up in a modest dress of midnight blue. He winked at her and then, as the music heralded the approach of the bride, Chay forgot everything else as Dana appeared in the doorway. Sheathed in a whisper of white satin, one hand on her father's arm, she moved gracefully toward him, her face radiant behind a gossamer veil, so beautiful she took his breath away.

"Who giveth this woman to be married to this man?"

"Her mother and I do," Mr. Westlake said, and placed Dana's hand in Chay's.

His fingers curled around hers.

Caught up in her beauty, Chay scarcely heard what the minister had to say until he came to the part where he asked if Chay would have Dana as his wife.

Chay nodded. "Yes." He cleared his throat. "Yes," he repeated.

"And do you, Dana Elizabeth Westlake, take Chayton Lone Elk to be your lawfully wedded husband?"

Dana squeezed Chay's hand. "Yes."

"Then by the power vested in me, and in the presence of this company, I now pronounce you man and wife. Chay, you may kiss your bride."

Dana's heart was pounding like a war drum as Chay lifted her veil.

"I love you, Mrs. Lone Elk," he murmured for her ears alone, and then he kissed her.

She had warned him about this kiss. It was to be short, just a shadow of a kiss, nothing outrageous. Apparently Chay hadn't listened. He took her in his arms and kissed her until her toes curled inside her shoes. Kissed her until muted laughter rolled through the church. Only then did he draw away.

Dana tried to glare at him but all she could do was smile.

The minister cleared his throat. "May I present Mr. and Mrs. Lone Elk, the newest couple in our fair city."

Chay took her by the hand and they walked down the aisle and out of the church. Once outside, Chay pulled her into his arms and kissed her again, and then, with a grin, he swung her into his arms and carried her down the stairs and into the waiting limo.

The driver shut the door and then Chay was drawing her into his arms once again.

"Just a quick kiss," Dana scolded. "You promised."

"I know," he said, nibbling on her earlobe, "but you didn't tell me you were going to look so beautifully irresistible."

"You were late," she said.

"I know, I'm sorry. Derek decided to take a shortcut and we had a flat. His spare wasn't in much better shape but we got as far as the gas station before it gave out. They didn't have a new tire that was the right size and it took some time to get the old one patched." He shook his head. "I was afraid you'd be long gone by the time I got to the church."

"Never. I knew you'd come. I never doubted it for a minute."

Chay caressed her cheek. "That's my girl."

The reception was everything Dana had ever dreamed of. Though the guests were few, they hadn't skimped on anything. The tables were set with crystal and fine china, there was food and champagne in abundance, soft drinks for the youth. When the meal was over and the tables moved to the edge of the floor, there was dancing.

Naturally, the bride and groom shared the first dance.

Dana moved into her husband's arms

feeling more confident, more beautiful, than she ever had in her whole life. Chay looked stunning in his tux. That wasn't surprising, since a tux did amazing things for even the most ordinary men, and Chay was far from ordinary. Just looking at him made her heart skip a beat. She could hardly wait until it was time for them to slip away. Just thinking of being alone with Chay brought a flush to her cheeks.

Later, Dana saw Ashley and Brandon dancing together. Dana smiled as Brandon twirled Ashley around the floor. It was good to see Chay's sister laughing and having a good time. Dana had always wanted a sister and she was glad that Ashley was staying at the ranch. It would give them a chance to get to know each other better.

She watched as Megan, LuAnn and Brittany clustered around Ashley and Brandon when the music ended. Dana smiled inwardly, thinking of the fun they would all have next summer, and how relieved Chay would be that he wouldn't have to act as chaperon.

The rest of the evening passed in a blur. They cut the cake. Her father made a toast to their happiness. Chay's mother also said a few words, her smile warm as she welcomed Dana into the family. Dana danced with her father while Chay danced with his mother.

And then, at last, it was time for them to go. Dana kissed her mom and dad goodbye, hugged Ashley and Claudia, and then she and Chay slipped out a side door to where the limo was waiting.

As soon as they were alone, Chay pulled her into his arms and kissed her, his hands moving over her back, across her breasts.

"Chay!" She glanced at the driver, wondering if he was watching them or the road.

"It's one-way glass," Chay said. "He can't see us."

"Are you sure?"

"I'm sure, darlin'," he said, his voice low and seductive. "Come here."

She lifted one eyebrow. "What do you want?"

"What do you think I want?"

"I truly don't know, sir," she said with mock innocence. "I've never been married before." She paused. "I've never been intimate with a man before."

But that was about to change. The thought sent a rush of heat spiraling to the deepest core of her being. She only hoped she wouldn't disappoint him. "Have you been with a lot of women?"

"A few," he admitted, "but they weren't you."

"Have you ever been in love before?" she asked, and wondered what perverse demon had made her ask such a question at such a time.

"I've been in serious lust a few times." He brushed his lips over the tip of her nose. "But I've never been in love. I know now I was waiting for you."

Sweet words that warmed her inside and out.

"We're here," he said as the limo pulled over to the curb in front of the Wardman Arms Hotel.

Like everything that carried the Wardman name, the hotel was first class all the way, from the etching on the glass doors to the expensive carpet in the lobby.

The driver opened the door for them. He winked at Chay, smiled at Dana, then opened the trunk and carried their bags inside.

Taking Dana by the hand, Chay led her into the hotel lobby and signed the register.

"Mr. and Mrs. Lone Elk," the clerk said, handing Chay a key. "I trust your stay will be a pleasant one. Your bags will be sent up to your room immediately."

Chay nodded his thanks. Dana gasped when Chay swung her into his arms and carried her across the lobby toward the elevator.

"I can walk."

"I know you can," he said amiably, "but I like this better."

Since it was useless to argue, she settled into his arms, her head resting on his shoulder. It was rather enjoyable, being held in the arms of a strong, handsome man.

Inside the elevator, he nuzzled her neck, sending shivers of anticipation racing down her spine.

He carried her down the hallway to their room, slipped the key card into the slot and carried her over the threshold.

"Here we are, Mrs. Lone Elk."

She nodded, feeling suddenly shy.

A knock at the door announced the arrival of their bags. Reluctantly Chay put her down and opened the door.

The bellboy put their bags in the bedroom, then pointed out the features of the room.

Chay tipped the young man and walked him to the door.

"Enjoy your stay," the young man said.

"If you need anything, just let me know."

Chay glanced at Dana. "I've got everything I need right here."

"Yes, sir!" the young man said, grinning, and closed the door.

"Now," Chay said, "where were we?"

"I believe you were about to kiss me."

"I believe you're right."

She smiled as he drew her into his arms.

"Did I tell you how beautiful you are, and how happy I am that you're my wife?"

"Not yet."

He chuckled softly. "You're beautiful, darlin', and I'm the luckiest man in the world."

"I think you're beautiful, too," she murmured.

"Handsome," he corrected.

"All right, handsome, if you insist."

"Enough talk," he said. And then he kissed her with all the love in his heart, and each kiss was a promise of forever.

"I need to get out of this dress," she said when he broke the kiss.

"Let me help you." He turned her around and began unfastening the back of her gown.

His fingertips were warm against her skin. He slipped the dress over her shoulders, let it fall to the floor, then turned her to face him again. "Beautiful!"

She flushed with pleasure and a hint of embarrassment at standing there clad in nothing but her underwear and high heels. "I'll be right back."

He nodded and she hurried into the bedroom to slip into her nightgown. It was long, white and sleeveless, and so sheer it was like wearing nothing at all.

When she returned to the other room, the look on Chay's face told her the gown had been worth the exorbitant price she had paid for it.

He whistled softly, his whole body coming alive at the sight of the vision standing before him. She looked like a naughty angel, innocent yet provocative, Eve before she bit the apple, Pandora before she opened the box.

"Well?" She tilted her head to one side.

"I'm speechless."

She smiled as she glided toward him, then tugged on his jacket. "Are you going to wear this to bed?"

Chay laughed as he shrugged out of his jacket and tossed it over a chair. His tie and shirt followed, then his shoes, socks and belt. Clad only in his trousers, he swung her into his arms and carried her into the bedroom.

Putting her on the bed, he began unfastening his trousers.

Dana's eyes widened. "Aren't you going to turn out the lights?"

"Do you want me to?"

She thought about it for the space of a heartbeat. "No." Wide-eyed, she watched him take off his pants. If she'd had any doubts about whether he wanted her or not, they were soon put to rest.

Still wearing his shorts, he slid into bed beside her and drew her into his arms. He showered her with warm, sweet kisses, murmuring that he loved her, adored her. Ah, the wonder of his kisses. Somehow, her nightgown disappeared and she reveled in the touch of his bare skin against hers.

Her fingertips glided across his broad chest, feathered over his strong, flat belly, as she marveled at the sheer beauty of the man. His skin was like copper, warm and smooth. His muscles rippled as she caressed him, making her stomach flutter. He let her explore his body to her heart's content, her hands moving a little lower each time until he obligingly removed his shorts. She found that part of him that made him a man as impressive as the rest.

He grinned, obviously pleased. And then he was touching her, his hands patient and gentle as he taught her that there was far more to intimacy than the act itself, that true love between a man and a woman was far more than the joining of passion-heated flesh. It was a uniting of hearts and souls and spirits, a coming together that was stronger than yearning, more enduring than desire.

She felt a soul-deep sense of rightness as their bodies merged and became one. She cried his name, her heart overflowing with wonder and delight as he took her to heights and depths she had never known existed. His clever hands aroused her until she writhed beneath him, yearning, reaching for something that remained just out of her reach until, at last, he carried her over the edge, and the world as she knew it shattered and became something new, something bright and more beautiful than anything she had ever imagined. She was floating on air, riding on a warm sea of sensual pleasure that crested and broke and crested again.

Breathless, unable to express what she was feeling in words, she held him close, her heart swelling with love and gratitude for this man, this moment.

She had never really believed in happy-ever-after, but now, curled in Chay's warm embrace, the ending she had once dreamed of became a reality.

Epilogue

Ashley shook her head when she entered the living room and found Dana and Chay sitting on the sofa, kissing. "Hello. Hello!"

Chay looked at her over the top of Dana's head. "Hello yourself."

"Do you two ever do anything but kiss?"

Chay glanced pointedly at the cradle beside the sofa where his seven-month-old daughter slept. "We make beautiful babies."

Ashley rolled her eyes. "That's what comes from all that kissing. Honestly, you'd think you two were still newlyweds."

Dana smiled. Though she and Chay had been married almost two years, she still felt like a new bride. Her pulse still raced when Chay entered the room. Her heart still swelled with love whenever she saw his smile or heard his voice. Each night in his arms was as wonderful and as exciting as the first time.

She loved being Chay's wife. She loved being a mother. She loved living on the ranch.

And she loved having Ashley and the girls underfoot for the summer. LuAnn, Megan and Brittany had arrived the week before and the house seemed to be in a constant state of activity, the air perpetually filled with the sound of feminine giggles and whispers. The girls all adored the baby and fought over whose turn it was to hold her. One good thing about a houseful of teenagers was that there was always a baby-sitter handy when she needed one. Dana had thought Ashley would want to spend her summers with her mother but Ashley didn't want to be away from the ranch that long. Instead, she went to see Jillian during Easter vacation and for a week at Christmas.

"I hate to bother you," Ashley said, "I just came to remind you that we're going to town with Brandon and some friends."

"Right," Chay said. "Don't be too late."

"Have a good time," Dana said. It was hard to believe that Ashley was almost eighteen, or that she was still seeing Brandon. Ashley dated other young men and Brandon dated other girls, but Dana had a feeling that the two of them were meant to be together. It would, she thought, be a good match.

And life was good, Dana mused as her husband kissed her again. So good, and it only promised to get better.

"Well, don't let me disturb you," Ashley said. "I'm sure Debra Ann would love to have a little brother."

Chay looked down at his wife and smiled. "Sounds like a good idea to me. What do you think?"

"I like it," she said, winking at him. "Let's talk about it later."

Chay nodded. "It's a date."

And later that night, they went upstairs to their room and locked the door.

So they could talk.

About the Author

Madeline Baker has written over twenty historical novels, half a dozen short stories under her own name and over seventeen paranormal novels under the name Amanda Ashley as well as Madeline Baker. Born and raised in California, she admits balancing her love for historical romance and vampires isn't easy — but she wouldn't like to choose between them. The award-winning author has now found another outlet for her writing — with Silhouette Romance! Readers can send a SASE to P. O. Box 1703, Whittier, CA 90609-1703 or visit her at her Web site www.madelinebaker.net.